A DUSK OF IDOLS

Previous Titles by this author from Severn House

A WORK OF ART

A DUSK OF IDOLS

and other stories

James Blish

edited by
Francis Lyall

This first world edition published in Great Britain 1996 by
SEVERN HOUSE PUBLISHERS LTD of
9–15 High Street, Sutton, Surrey SM1 1DF.
First published in the USA 1996 by
SEVERN HOUSE PUBLISHERS INC of
595 Madison Avenue, New York, NY 10022.

British Library Cataloguing in Publication Data
Blish, James
    A dusk of idols
    1. American fiction – 20th century
    I. Title
    813.5'4 [F]

    ISBN 0-7278-4967-0

Typeset by Hewer Text Composition Services, Edinburgh.
Printed and bound in Great Britain by
Hartnolls Ltd, Bodmin, Cornwall.

Contents

Introduction

The best writers have an identifiable individuality, a quality of style that is personal to them, that makes their work unmistakable. In a sense a writer's name is a brand name, giving an assurance of quality and often a probability of type of content. Out of their experience readers develop a liking that can amount to a loyalty to a writer; in other cases the sight of a name on the spine of a book on the shelf will lead one to move on – fast.

I hope some read this Introduction because they are familiar with James Blish from *A Work of Art and Other Stories*, the collection of his shorter work published in 1993. Others will certainly know his magnificent novels. For them the name 'James Blish' is the reason for picking up this book. It will come into the hands of yet others for many reasons. For some curiosity may be triggered by the cover or the title. It may be a borrow. It may even come as a gift from a discerning friend. Those who do not know the author already will like what they read and seek out more, or will decide that 'Blish' is not for them. One thing is clear: indifference is a rare option. You either like 'Blish' or you do not.

As a writer James Blish is a distinctive voice within sf. There is a refreshing sharpness about the content and the execution of his stories. In part this stems from another of his talents. Apart from his status as an author, through his criticism James Blish was one of the shapers of modern sf. As William Atheling, Jr. (an oblique tribute to Ezra Pound,

1

one of his own heroes) Blish secured a reputation for honest and trenchant criticism of science fiction that did much to raise standards of writing in the genre in the 1950s and 1960s. His criticism, collected during his life in *The Issue at Hand* (1964), and *More Issues at Hand* (1970) (both from Advent:Publishers of Chicago), was followed in 1987 by *The Tale that Wags the God* (edited by Cy Chauvin, with a complete bibliography compiled by Judith Blish) also from Advent:Publishers. These books are still worth seeking out. But the articles had an immediate as well as a lasting value. They were first published in the magazines and fanzines, and therefore were read by authors (discussed and others) while they were still writing. They were also read by editors – the first hurdle between an author and the public. The articles identified faults and failings among the sf writers of the time. Sloppy thought, language or plot construction, in varying combinations, were revealed. But Blish did not indulge himself in his criticism. He was not motivated by hostility or jealousy. He was no tender ego bolstering itself by miscalling the work of others. Blish was always intent on what he called technical criticism. His aim was to help authors improve. The more thin-skinned recipients of his honesty could find him waspish, but most learned, as did those who could see the faults he highlighted appearing in their own, lesser, work. The editors took note too.

James Blish and a few others, particularly his friend the late Damon Knight (see the first and second editions of Knight's *In Search of Wonder*, Advent: Publishers, Chicago, 1956 and 1967) therefore helped raise the standard of sf writing, laying a foundation of expectation that led to the present day high standards, particularly among 'hard sf'.

James Blish was not only a critic. He was concerned to encourage and train as well as to exhort and identify lapses from high standards. Writing is partially a gift, but a good deal of it is craft, and craft – the mechanics of authorship – can be analysed, and major elements of its practice explained and revealed to would-be practitioners. An apprenticeship, learning from someone more experienced, can help develop a writer's talent. Blish gained greatly from a period spent as a literary agent's reader, analysing and diagnosing the faults of hundreds of manuscripts, and thereby he learned the elements of many sorts of literary craftsmanship. He contributed that expertise as one of the founders and tutelary spirits of the Milford Science Fiction Writers Conference. That annual workshop at Milford, Pennsylvania, did much to bring on a younger generation of authors, and indeed benefited the whole sf industry by birthing the Science Fiction Writers of America (SFWA). When Blish came to Britain in 1969 he showed a similar concern, and in 1971 was one of those instrumental in the setting up of the Science Fiction Foundation.

Blish was born in 1921 and grew up in East Orange, New Jersey. His mother taught piano, which left him with an enduring love of music both as an art and as a language, a feature that can be seen in some of his stories. He, however, first sought a career in science and studied biology at Rutgers University, an interest that manifests in a goodly number of his stories. At Rutgers he was introduced to some of the basic questions of epistemology – how do we know what we know? Can knowledge be trusted? – themes that preoccupied him for the rest of his life. After graduation he was drafted into service in the US Army for two years as a medical laboratory technician, during which he wrote nothing. He returned to graduate school at Columbia University, but also returned to authorship – not only science fiction, but sports, westerns, detectives and thrillers as well. He also wrote poetry, and a book of his poems, *With All of Love*, was published in 1995, by Aramnesis Press, San Francisco, US.

But, for most, authorship is not a stable occupation. After a brief period as a full-time author in 1948 Blish found he had to make his living as a science writer and public relations executive, writing stories during his lunch hours, evenings, weekends. It was not until 1969 that he was able to retire from corporate life and move to Henley-on-Thames, near Oxford. But even by then he was in ill-health. He died of cancer on 30 July 1975 and is buried in the cemetery of St Cross Church, Oxford. His biographer, David Ketterer, tells us that at the committal his English editor, Charles Monteith, read the *Lament for the Makaris* by Gavin Dunbar (*c*.1460 – before 1522). It fits. (See D. Ketterer, *Imprisoned in a Tesseract: The Life and Work of James Blish*, Kent, Ohio: Kent State UP, 1987, at 28).

Whatever occupation was paying the bills – and he did not stint on that necessary work – Blish was an author. His output includes hundreds of short stories, of which the small sample here can give but a taste, and that only in the sf genre. Some of his best stories appear first in the sf magazines, but later turn up as integral parts of novels, or were expanded into novels. With the exception of 'Beep' for the reason given below, I have not as yet considered stories that Blish himself later used for inclusion in a collection. Perhaps that is wrong, for several stand well as shorts. Perhaps in the future . . . But if this sample of short stories intrigues, seek out among his twenty-three novels the *Cities in Flight* tetralogy, a real space epic (1970, reissued in the UK 1991, consisting of *They Shall Have Stars*, 1956, US title *Year 2018!; A Life for the Stars*, 1962; *Earthman Come Home*, 1955; and *A Clash of Cymbals* 1958, US title *The Triumph of Time*). There is also the magnificent sequence which, after he had finished the first three elements, he was intrigued to recognise form a trilogy. He dubbed it *After Such Knowledge* – a quotation of the T.S. Eliot line that ends, '. . . what forgiveness?' The link between the several elements is that the stories in different ways raise but do not answer the question whether the desire for secular knowledge is a misuse of the mind – an evil, even. The first published was the Hugo winning *A Case of Conscience* (novel version 1958) about a Catholic priest who confronts a profound spiritual question and then decision in the future. Over the years it has fascinated many, and triggered much

4

discussion, not to say speculation. The second published was *Doctor Mirabilis* (1964), a biographical novel about Roger Bacon, a thirteenth century prototype of the anxious relationship between science and faith. The third was *Black Easter* (1968) to which he added *The Day After Judgement* (1970). Considered by Blish himself as one work, these latter two were most recently republished together as *The Devil's Day* (Baen Books, 1990). All four (three?) were published in the UK in 1991 in one volume under Blish's chosen title *After Such Knowledge*, and are there arranged in the order Blish himself preferred: *Doctor Mirabilis, Black Easter, The Day After Judgement* and *A Case of Conscience*.

But it would not do to give the impression that Blish was one of those unduly blinkered, 'serious' authors. Apart from the occasional humorous short, there is the novelisation of the first eleven Star Trek stories (though much of the last six is to be attributed to Judith Blish), and the separate *Spock Must Die* (1970) all of which gave (and gives) pleasure to a juvenile audience. Indeed, the glad reception a young audience gave the Star Trek novels gave James Blish great satisfaction.

Like its predecessor, this collection attempts to give a flavour of the range of Blish's sf writing. It spans a fourteen year period of publication from 'Mistake Inside' of 1948 to 'A Dusk of Idols' of 1961. That was a time when there were worries of international conflict, worries which come through in some of these stories. Collectors will know that certain of the stories have appeared in other collections, including Blish's own *Galactic Cluster* (1959, US: abridged, 1960, UK) and *Anywhen* (1970, US: 1971, UK) and in R.A.W. Lowndes, ed., *The Best of James Blish* (1979, Del Rey/Ballantine). But these volumes are not now readily available, and there is a new generation to discover 'James Blish'.

Such new readers will discover someone who is by no means always a 'soothing read', chewing gum for the eyes. There is often a deft fingering of a nerve, a jog to thought and to accepted attitudes. Frequently there is an ambiguity in the resolution of a story, designed to make you think, or feel. The story may have concluded, but it is not ended. As noted above, many of these stories reflect the problems of their time, and it is disturbing to find they remain relevant.

'To Pay the Piper' appeared early in 1956, the year of Suez and of the Hungarian Rising and its suppression. War felt near then, and biological weaponry was not unthinkable. This tale of treachery and sabotage reveals Blish's scientific background, as well as ringing a wry variation on the root of its title. Perhaps twenty years underground existence seems fanciful now that the Communist bloc has collapsed, but there has been recent talk of biological weapons as the Poor Man's A-bomb, and missile delivery systems are becoming readily available thanks to the economic crises of a large part of the world. Not a pleasant thought!

'Beep' (1954) is one of Blish's most famous stories and was published soon after 'Common Time' (1953) (included in the previous collection). For the author to have produced two such gems in swift sequence is remarkable, but when one realises that the first appearance of the initial short story version of 'A Case of Conscience' was also in 1953 one's astonishment increases. And if one traces the story seeds that Blish seems to have set in the six year period of the early 1950s, it overflows. Like *A Case of Conscience* (novel, 1958), 'Beep' was to be expanded, but *The Quincunx of Time* (1973), perhaps showing the effect of his fatal cancer, takes the story no further, and I have to say that I prefer this version – that is why it is included!

Like a good many sf stories, the appeal of 'Beep' lies more in the ideas it contains rather than the detail of plot or character. It is a 'Time' story, which also re-examines the old 'freewill v determinism' argument and comes to a thought provoking conclusion. Were we to discover the secret of 'Beep', would the result be the one adopted by our successors of that far future? Or, would the matter be tested – of course in the purest interests of scientific inquiry? And would we *know* the result? As noted above, such questions of knowledge and how we know what we know were matters that preoccupied Blish.

'The Box' (1949) is an early story which Blish himself liked enough to reprint in his own first anthology, *So Close to Home* (1961). New York wakes to find itself cut off inside a barrier – a concept found in many early pulp stories. But although there are traces of the pulp in it – the thousands that die along the periphery – this story treats the idea differently. The protagonist is a former inmate of a Nazi concentration camp, who nonetheless comes to be suspected by the military mind, even as he solves the puzzle and deals with the threat. Further, although there is an element of flim-flam in the science, it is well done flim-flam, the sort that a reader is quite willing to put up with so long as the rest of the tale satisfies.

'The Writing of the Rat' comes both in contrast and in parallel with its predecessor. Again, as in many Blish stories of the 40s and 50s, there is an anger against the practitioners of war, and the awfulness that war engenders. There is also an intellectual somersault to be performed by the reader. And, as in a number of Blish's stories, the reader is then left with an ambiguous resolution: will the revelation of the true nature of humanity have the effect that the protagonists hope?

Like 'To Pay the Piper', the next story, 'The King of the Hill' (1955), comes from tense times. In the 1950s there were real worries whether those in charge of the final processes of nuclear response were sufficiently stable, and various authors considered the matter. But the concern was shared by government and the military. As we now know, double keying and other procedures were devised to minimise the chances of accidental war. 'The King of the Hill' is Blish's own view. Its technology is obsolete – the teletype, the orbital placement of SV1, and the ease with which Harris gets to it are all, we now know, wrong. But the basic idea is right. And the twisting of the end is typical Blish, inserting an ambiguity that comes back to epistemology. How much of what we hear is bluff; would it be good to know truth; and how would we know we were actually and accurately distinguishing the one from the other?

'A Matter of Energy' (also 1955) shows Blish's ability both to amuse and to parody. The 'target' or perhaps better the 'trigger' for the story is L. Sprague de Camp's famous *Lest Darkness Fall* (1949), where Martin Padway, projected to the Roman Empire of the sixth century uses his limited technical knowledge, his wits and recollection of the past as he had known it to alter the course of history. See how it is altered in this tale! And note also the running gag: all authors have trouble with writing dialogue – you cannot just say 'he said' all the time!

'Mistake Inside' (1948) is the earliest story in this collection. Published first under the pseudonym of 'Arthur Merlyn' (not inappropriately given the content) the story is a romp through the debatable land between science and the occult. Reading it one is reminded of the later flowering of similar notions in *Black Easter* (1968) and *The Day After Judgement* (1970), even to the mention of Dis (though the poetic reference to Dirac should also be noted – perhaps a link to 'Beep'). In its hints as to mental powers, it also chimes in with other work that Blish had in hand at the time, notably 'Let the Finder Beware', which was to be extended into the novel *Jack of Eagles* (1952), his first solo novel.

'A Dusk of Idols' (1961) is different. The title comes from Nietzsche's book of the same name. The tale is one of mysterious, slow horror, mediated in the traditional way through having a narrator recount the events that happened to another. The story is therefore 'third-party' to the reader, lending a distancing as well as an ambiguity, for the intermediary does not know everything, though he knows more than the reader. In skilled hands, as in this case, the device can be very effective. Without in any way implying there is a connection, 'A Dusk' reminds me of Ursula Le Guin's

'The Ones That Walk Away From Omelas' (1973; in *The Wind's Twelve Quarters*, vol.2, 1976, 112–120). Is there not a truth that some societies seem to survive through losing the less fit among them? And where does that leave certain modern societies? Or, more blackly, is it not true that, as Naysmith says, death is the drive wheel of evolution? This story picks up an additional resonance when we remember its author was to die comparatively young.

Blish was fifty-four when he died. He left a large body of work, certain of which are acknowledged classics in the field. One wonders wistfully what his fertile mind might have conjured had he been granted longer. The two linked sequences, *Cities in Flight* and *After Such Knowledge*, are the major foundations of his present reputation, but the stories in this collection show his versatility at the shorter lengths. Enjoy them.

F. Lyall

Aberdeen, Scotland,
January 1996.

To Pay the Piper

The man in the white jacket stopped at the door marked *Re-Education Project–Col. H. H. Mudgett, Commanding Officer* and waited while the scanner looked him over. He had been through that door a thousand times, but the scanner made as elaborate a job of it as if it had never seen him before.

It always did, for there was always in fact a chance that it *had* never seen him before, whatever the fallible human beings to whom it reported might think. It went over him from gray, crew-cut poll to reagent-proof shoes, checking his small wiry body and lean profile against its stored silhouettes, tasting and smelling him as dubiously as if he were an orange held in storage two days too long.

"Name?" it said at last.

"Carson, Samuel, 32–454–0698."

"Business?"

"Medical director, Re-Ed One."

While Carson waited, a distant, heavy concussion came rolling down upon him through the mile of solid granite above his head. At the same moment, the letters on the door – and everything else inside his cone of vision – blurred distressingly, and a stab of pure pain went lancing through his head. It was the supersonic component of the explosion, and it was harmless – except that it always both hurt and scared him.

The light on the door-scanner, which had been glowing yellow up to now, flicked back to red again and the machine began the whole routine all over; the sound bomb had reset it. Carson patiently endured its inspection, gave his name, serial number, and mission once more, and this time got the green. He went in, unfolding as he walked the flimsy square of cheap paper he had been carrying all along.

Mudgett looked up from his desk and said at once: "What now?"

The physician tossed the square of paper down under Mudgett's eyes. "Summary of the press reaction to Hamelin's speech last night," he said. "The total effect is going against us, Colonel. Unless we can change Hamelin's mind, this outcry to re-educate civilians ahead of soldiers is going to lose the war for us. The urge to live on the surface again has been mounting for ten years; now it's got a target to focus on. Us."

Mudgett chewed on a pencil while he read the summary; a blocky, bulky man, as short as Carson and with hair as gray and close-cropped. A year ago, Carson would have told him that nobody in Re-Ed could afford to put stray objects in his mouth even once, let alone as a habit; now Carson just waited. There wasn't a man – or a woman or a child – of America's surviving thirty-five million 'sane' people who didn't have some such tic. Not now, not after twenty-five years of underground life.

"He knows it's impossible, doesn't he?" Mudgett demanded abruptly.

"Of course he doesn't," Carson said impatiently. "He doesn't know any more about the real nature of the project than the people do. He thinks the 'educating' we do is in some sort of survival technique . . . That's what the papers think, too, as you can plainly see by the way they loaded that editorial."

"Um. If we'd taken direct control of the papers in the first place . . ."

Carson said nothing. Military control of every facet of civilian life was a fact, and Mudgett knew it. He also knew that an appearance of freedom to think is a necessity for the human mind – and that the appearance could not be maintained without a few shreds of the actuality.

"Suppose we do this," Mudgett said at last. "Hamelin's position in the State Department makes it impossible for us to muzzle him. But it ought to be possible to explain to him that no unprotected human being can live on the surface, no matter how many Merit Badges he had for woodcraft and first aid. Maybe we could even take him on a little trip topside; I'll wager he's never seen it."

"And what if he dies up there?" Carson said stonily. "We lose three-fifths of every topside party as it is – and Hamelin's an inexperienced —"

"Might be the best thing, mightn't it?"

"*No*," Carson said. "It would look like we'd planned it that way. The papers would have the populace boiling by the next morning."

Mudgett groaned and nibbled another double row of indentations around the barrel of the pencil. "There must be something," he said.

"There is."

"Well?"

"Bring the man here and show him just what we *are* doing. Re-educate *him*, if necessary. Once we told the newspapers that he'd taken the course . . . well, who knows, they just might resent it. Abusing his clearance privileges and so on."

"We'd be violating our basic policy," Mudgett said slowly. "'Give the Earth back to the men who fight for it.' Still, the idea has some merits . . ."

"Hamelin is out in the antechamber right now," Carson said. "Shall I bring him in?"

The radioactivity never did rise much beyond a mildly hazardous level, and that was only transient, during the second week of the war – the week called the Death of Cities. The small shards of sanity retained by the high commands on both sides dictated avoiding weapons with a built-in backfire; no cobalt bombs were dropped, no territories

13

permanently poisoned. Generals still remembered that unoccupied territory, no matter how devastated, is still unconquered territory.

But no such considerations stood in the way of biological warfare. It was controllable: you never released against the enemy any disease you didn't yourself know how to control. There would be some slips, of course, but the margin for error . . .

There were some slips. But for the most part, biological warfare worked fine. The great fevers washed like tides around and around the globe, one after another. In such cities as had escaped the bombings, the rumble of truck convoys carrying the puffed heaped corpses to the mass graves became the only sound except for sporadic small-arms fire; and then that too ceased, and the trucks stood rusting in rows.

Nor were human beings the sole victims. Cattle fevers were sent out. Wheat rusts, rice molds, corn blights, hog choleras, poultry enteritises, fountained into the indifferent air from the hidden laboratories, or were loosed far aloft, in the jet-stream, by rocketing fleets. Gelatin capsules pullulating with gill-rots fell like hail into the great fishing grounds of New-foundland, Oregon, Japan, Sweden, Portugal. Hundreds of species of animals were drafted as secondary hosts for human diseases, were injected and released to carry the blessings of the laboratories to their mates and litters. It was discovered that minute amounts of the tetracycline series of antibiotics, which had long been used as feed supplements to bring farm animals to full market weight early, could also be used to raise the most whopping Anopheles and Aëdes mosquitoes anybody ever saw, capable of flying long distances against the wind and of carrying a peculiarly interesting new strain of the malarial parasite and the yellow fever virus . . .

By the time it had ended, everyone who remained alive was a mile under ground.

For good.

*   *   *

14

"I still fail to understand why," Hamelin said, "if, as you claim, you have methods of re-educating soldiers for surface life, you can't do so for civilians as well. Or instead."

The Under Secretary, a tall, spare man, bald on top, and with a heavily creased forehead, spoke with the odd neutral accent – untinged by regionalism – of the trained diplomat, despite the fact that there had been no such thing as a foreign service for nearly half a century.

"We're going to try to explain that to you," Carson said. "But we thought that, first of all, we'd try to explain once more why we think it would be bad policy – as well as physically out of the question.

"Sure, everybody wants to go topside as soon as it's possible. Even people who are reconciled to these endless caverns and corridors hope for something better for their children – a glimpse of sunlight, a little rain, the fall of a leaf. That's more important now to all of us than the war, which we don't believe in any longer. That doesn't even make any military sense, since we haven't the numerical strength to occupy the enemy's territory any more, and they haven't the strength to occupy ours. We understand all that. But we also know that the enemy is intent on prosecuting the war to the end. Extermination is what they say they want, on their propaganda broadcasts, and your own Department reports that they seem to mean what they say. So we can't give up fighting them; that would be simple suicide. Are you still with me?"

"Yes, but I don't see —"

"Give me a moment more. If we have to continue to fight, we know this much: that the first of the two sides to get men on the surface again – so as to be able to *attack* important targets, not just keep them isolated in seas of plagues – will be the side that will bring this war to an end. They know that, too. We have good reason to believe that they have a re-education project, and that it's about as far advanced as ours is."

"Look at it this way," Colonel Mudgett burst in unexpectedly. "What we have now is a stalemate. A saboteur occasionally locates one of the underground cities and lets the pestilences into it. Sometimes on our side, sometimes on theirs. But that only happens sporadically, and it's just more of this mutual extermination business – to which we're committed, willy-nilly, for as long as they are. If we can get troops onto the surface first, we'll be able to scout out their important installations in short order, and issue them a surrender ultimatum with teeth in it. They'll take it. The only other course is the sort of slow, mutual suicide we've got now."

Hamelin put the tips of his fingers together. "You gentlemen lecture me about policy as if I had never heard the word before. I'm familiar with your arguments for sending soldiers first. You assume that you're familiar with all of mine for starting with civilians, but you're wrong, because some of them haven't been brought up at all outside the Department. I'm going to tell you some of them, and I think they'll merit your close attention."

Carson shrugged. "I'd like nothing better than to be convinced, Mr. Secretary. Go ahead."

"You of all people should know, Dr. Carson, how close our underground society is to a psychotic break. To take a single instance, the number of juvenile gangs roaming these corridors of ours has increased 400 per cent since the rumor about the Re-Education Project began to spread. Or another: the number of individual crimes without motive – crimes committed just to distract the committer from the grinding monotony of the life we all lead – has now passed the total of all other crimes put together.

"And as for actual insanity – of our thirty-five million people still unhospitalized, there are four million cases *of which we know*, each one of which should be committed right now for early paranoid schizophrenia – except that

16

were we to commit them, our essential industries would suffer a manpower loss more devastating than anything the enemy has inflicted upon us. Every one of those four million persons is a major hazard to his neighbors and to his job, but how can we do without them? And what can we do about the unrecognized, subclinical cases, which probably total twice as many? How long can we continue operating without a collapse under such conditions?"

Carson mopped his brow. "I didn't suspect that it had gone that far."

"It has gone that far," Hamelin said icily, "and it is accelerating. Your own project has helped to accelerate it. Colonel Mudgett here mentioned the opening of isolated cities to the pestilences. Shall I tell you how Louisville fell?"

"A spy again, I suppose," Mudgett said.

"No, Colonel. Not a spy. A band of – of vigilantes, of mutineers. I'm familiar with your slogan, 'The Earth to those who fight for it.' Do you know the counterslogan that's circulating among the people?"

They waited. Hamelin smiled and said: "'Let's die on the surface.'"

"They overwhelmed the military detachment there, put the city administration to death, and blew open the shaft to the surface. About a thousand people actually made it to the top. Within twenty-four hours the city was dead – as the ring-leaders had been warned would be the outcome. The warning didn't deter them. Nor did it protect the prudent citizens who had no part in the affair."

Hamelin leaned forward suddenly. "People won't wait to be told when it's their turn to be re-educated. They'll be tired of waiting, tired to the point of insanity of living at the bottom of a hole. They'll just go.

"And that, gentlemen, will leave the world to the enemy . . . or, more likely, the rats. They alone are immune to everything by now."

There was a long silence. At last Carson said mildly: "Why aren't *we* immune to everything by now?"

"Eh? Why – the new generations. They've never been exposed."

"We still have a reservoir of older people who lived through the war: people who had one or several of the new diseases that swept the world, some as many as five, and yet recovered. They still have their immunities. We know; we've tested them. We know from sampling that no new disease has been introduced by either side in over ten years now. Against all the known ones, we have immunization techniques, anti-sera, antibiotics, and so on. I suppose you get your shots every six months like all the rest of us; we should all be very hard to infect now, and such infections as do take should run mild courses." Carson held the Under Secretary's eyes grimly. "Now, answer me this question: why is it that, despite all these protections, *every single person* in an opened city dies?"

"I don't know," Hamelin said, staring at each of them in turn. "By your showing some of them should recover."

"They should," Carson said. "But nobody does. Why? Because the very nature of disease has changed since we all went underground. There are now abroad in the world a number of mutated bacterial strains which can by-pass the immunity mechanisms of the human body altogether. What this means in simple terms is that, should such a germ get into your body, your body wouldn't recognize it as an invader. It would manufacture no antibodies against the germ. Consequently, the germ could multiply without any check, and – you would die. So would we all."

"I see," Hamelin said. He seemed to have recovered his composure extraordinarily rapidly. "I am no scientist, gentlemen, but what you tell me makes our position sound perfectly hopeless. Yet obviously you have some answer."

Carson nodded. "We do. But it's important for you to understand the situation, otherwise the answer will mean nothing to you. So: is it perfectly clear to you now, from

18

what we've said so far, that no amount of re-educating a man's brain, be he soldier *or* civilian, will allow him to survive on the surface?"

"Quite clear," Hamelin said, apparently ungrudgingly. Carson's hopes rose by a fraction of a millimeter. "But if you don't re-educate his brain, what can you re-educate? His reflexes, perhaps?"

"No," Carson said. "His lymph nodes, and his spleen."

A scornful grin began to appear on Hamelin's thin lips. "You need better public relations counsel than you've been getting," he said. "If what you say is true – as of course I assume it is – then the term 're-educate' is not only inappropriate, it's downright misleading. If you had chosen a less suggestive and more accurate label in the beginning, I wouldn't have been able to cause you half the trouble I have."

"I agree that we were badly advised there," Carson said. "But not entirely for those reasons. Of course the name is misleading; that's both a characteristic and a function of the names of top secret projects. But in this instance the name 'Re-Education,' bad as it now appears, subjected the men who chose it to a fatal temptation. You see, though it is misleading, it is also entirely accurate."

"Word games," Hamelin said.

"Not at all," Mudgett interposed. "We were going to spare you the theoretical reasoning behind our project, Mr. Secretary, but now you'll just have to sit still for it. The fact is that the body's ability to distinguish between its own cells and those of some foreign tissue – a skin graft, say, or a bacterial invasion of the blood – isn't an inherited ability. It's a learned reaction. Furthermore, if you'll think about it a moment, you'll see that it has to be. Body cells die, too, and have to be disposed of; what would happen if removing those dead cells provoked an antibody reaction, as the destruction of foreign cells does? We'd die of anaphylactic shock while we were still infants.

"For that reason, the body has to learn how to scavenge

19

selectively. In human beings, that lesson isn't learned completely until about a month after birth. During the intervening time, the newborn infant is protected by antibodies that it gets from the colestrum, the 'first milk' it gets from the breast during the three or four days immediately after birth. It can't generate its own; it isn't allowed to, so to speak, until it's learned the trick of cleaning up body residues *without* triggering the antibody mechanisms. Any dead cells marked 'personal' have to be dealt with some other way."

"That seems clear enough," Hamelin said. "But I don't see its relevance."

"Well, we're in a position now where that differentiation between the self and everything outside the body doesn't do us any good any more. These mutated bacteria have been 'selfed' by the mutation. In other words, some of their protein molecules, probably desoxyribonucleic acid molecules, carry configurations or 'recognition units' identical with those of our body cells, so that the body can't tell one from another."

"But what has all this to do with re-education?"

"Just this," Carson said. "What we do here is to impose upon the cells of the body – all of them – a new set of recognition units for the guidance of the lymph nodes and the spleen, which are the organs that produce antibodies. The new units are highly complex, and the chances of their being duplicated by bacterial evolution, even under forced draft, are too small to worry about. That's what Re-Education is. In a few moments, if you like, we'll show you just how it's done."

Hamelin ground out his fifth cigarette in Mudgett's ash tray and placed the tips of his fingers together thoughtfully. Carson wondered just how much of the concept of recognition-marking the Under Secretary had absorbed. It had to be admitted that he was astonishingly quick to take hold of abstract ideas, but the self-marker theory of immunity was – like everything else in immunology –

almost impossible to explain to laymen, no matter how intelligent.

"This process," Hamelin said hesitantly, "it takes a long time?"

"About six hours per subject, and we can handle only one man at a time. That means that we can count on putting no more than seven thousand troops into the field by the turn of the century. Every one will have to be a highly trained specialist, if we're to bring the war to a quick conclusion."

"Which means no civilians," Hamelin said. "I see. I'm not entirely convinced, but – by all means let's see how it's done."

Once inside, the Under Secretary tried his best to look everywhere at once. The room cut into the rock was roughly two hundred feet high. Most of it was occupied by the bulk of the Re-Education Monitor, a mechanism as tall as a fifteen-story building, and about a city block square. Guards watched it on all sides, and the face of the machine swarmed with technicians.

"Incredible," Hamelin murmured. "That enormous object can process only one man at a time?"

"That's right," Mudgett said. "Luckily it doesn't have to treat all the body cells directly. It works through the blood, re-selfing the cells by means of small changes in the serum chemistry."

"What kind of changes?"

"Well," Carson said, choosing each word carefully, "that's more or less a graveyard secret, Mr. Secretary. We can tell you this much: the machine uses a vast array of crystalline, complex sugars which *behave* rather like the blood-group-and-type proteins. They're fed into the serum in minute amounts, under feedback control of second-by-second analysis of the blood. The computations involved in deciding upon the amount and the precise nature of each introduced chemical are highly complex. Hence the size of the machine. It is, in its major effect, an artificial kidney."

"I've seen artificial kidneys in the hospitals," Hamelin said, frowning. "They're rather compact affairs."

"Because all they do is remove waste products from the patient's blood, and restore the fluid and electrolyte balance. Those are very minor renal functions in the higher mammals. The organ's main duty is chemical control of immunity. If Burnet and Fenner had known that back in 1949, when the selfing theory was being formulated, we'd have had Re-Education long before now."

"Most of the machine's size is due to the computation section," Mudgett emphasized. "In the body, the brain stem does those computations, as part of maintaining homeostasis. But we can't reach the brain stem from outside; it's not under conscious control. Once the body is re-selfed, it will retrain the thalamus where we can't." Suddenly, two swinging doors at the base of the machine were pushed apart and a mobile operating table came through, guided by two attendants. There was a form on it, covered to the chin with a sheet. The face above this sheet was immobile and almost as white.

Hamelin watched the table go out of the huge cavern with visibly mixed emotions. He said: "This process – it's painful?"

"No, not exactly," Carson said. The motive behind the question interested him hugely, but he didn't dare show it. "But any fooling around with the immunity mechanisms can give rise to symptoms – fever, general malaise, and so on. We try to protect our subjects by giving them a light shock anesthesia first."

"Shock?" Hamelin repeated. "You mean electroshock? I don't see how —"

"Call it stress anesthesia instead. We give the man a steroid drug that counterfeits the anesthesia the body itself produces in moments of great stress – on the battlefield, say, or just after a serious injury. It's fast, and free of aftereffects.

22

There's no secret about that, by the way; the drug involved is 21-hydroxypregnane-3, 20-dione sodium succinate, and it dates all the way back to 1955."

"Oh," the Under Secretary said. The ringing sound of the chemical name had had, as Carson had hoped, a ritually soothing effect.

"Gentlemen," Hamelin said hesitantly. "Gentlemen, I have a – a rather unusual request. And, I am afraid, a rather selfish one." A brief, nervous laugh. "Selfish in both senses, if you will pardon me the pun. You need feel no hesitation in refusing me, but —"

Abruptly he appeared to find it impossible to go on. Carson mentally crossed his fingers and plunged in.

"You would like to undergo the process yourself?" he said.

"Well, yes. Yes, that's exactly it. Does that seem inconsistent? I should know, should I not, what it is that I'm advocating for my following? Know it intimately, from personal experience, not just theory? Of course I realize that it would conflict with your policy, but I assure you I wouldn't turn it to any political advantage – none whatsoever. And perhaps it wouldn't be too great a lapse of policy to process just one civilian among your seven thousand soldiers."

Subverted, by God! Carson looked at Mudgett with a firmly straight face. It wouldn't do to accept too quickly.

But Hamelin was rushing on, almost chattering now. "I can understand your hesitation. You must feel that I'm trying to gain some advantage, or even to get to the surface ahead of my fellow men. If it will set your minds at rest, I would be glad to enlist in your advance army. Before five years are up, I could surely learn some technical skill which would make me useful to the expedition. If you would prepare papers to that effect, I'd be happy to sign them."

"That's hardly necessary," Mudgett said. "After you're Re-Educated, we can simply announce the fact, and say that you've agreed to join the advance party when the time comes."

"Ah," Hamelin said. "I see the difficulty. No, that would make my position quite impossible. If there is no other way . . ."

"Excuse us a moment," Carson said. Hamelin bowed, and the doctor pulled Mudgett off out of earshot.

"Don't overplay it," he murmured. "You're tipping our hand with that talk about a press release, Colonel. He's offering us a bribe – but he's plenty smart enough to see that the price you're suggesting is that of his whole political career; he won't pay that much."

"What then?" Mudgett whispered hoarsely.

"Get somebody to prepare the kind of informal contract he suggested. Offer to put it under security seal so we won't be able to show it to the press at all. He'll know well enough that such a seal can be broken if our policy ever comes before a presidential review – and that will restrain him from forcing such a review. Let's not demand too much. Once he's been Re-Educated, he'll have to live the rest of the five years with the knowledge that he *can* live topside any time he wants to try it – and he hasn't had the discipline our men have had. It's my bet that he'll goof off before the five years are up – and good riddance."

They went back to Hamelin, who was watching the machine and humming in a painfully abstracted manner.

"I've convinced the Colonel," Carson said, "that your services in the army might well be very valuable when the time comes, Mr. Secretary. If you'll sign up, we'll put the papers under security seal for your own protection, and then I think we can fit you into our treatment program today."

"I'm grateful to you, Dr. Carson," Hamelin said. "Very grateful indeed."

Five minutes after his injection, Hamelin was as peaceful as a flounder and was rolled through the swinging doors. An

24

hour's discussion of the probable outcome, carried on in the privacy of Mudgett's office, bore very little additional fruit, however.

"It's our only course," Carson said. "It's what we hoped to gain from his visit, duly modified by circumstances. It all comes down to this: Hamelin's compromised himself, and he knows it."

"But," Mudgett said, "suppose he was right? What about all that talk of his about mass insanity?"

"I'm sure it's true," Carson said, his voice trembling slightly despite his best efforts at control. "It's going to be rougher than ever down here for the next five years, Colonel. Our only consolation is that the enemy must have exactly the same problem; and if we can beat them to the surface —"

"*Hsst!*" Mudgett said. Carson had already broken off his sentence. He wondered why the scanner gave a man such a hard time outside that door, and then admitted him without any warning to the people on the other side. Couldn't the damned thing be trained to knock?

The newcomer was a page from the haemotology section. "Here's the preliminary rundown on your 'student X,' Dr. Carson," he said.

The page saluted Mudgett and went out. Carson began to read. After a moment, he also began to sweat.

"Colonel, look at this. I was wrong after all. Disastrously wrong. I haven't seen a blood-type distribution pattern like Hamelin's since I was a medical student, and even back then it was only a demonstration, not a real live patient. Look at it from the genetic point of view – the migration factors."

He passed the protocol across the desk. Mudgett was not by background a scientist, but he was an enormously able administrator, of the breed that makes it its business to know the technicalities on which any project ultimately rests. He was not much more than halfway through the tally before his eyebrows were gaining altitude like shock waves.

25

"Carson, we can't let that man into the machine! He's—"

"He's already in it, Colonel, you know that. And if we interrupt the process before it runs to term, we'll kill him."

"Let's kill him, then," Mudgett said harshly. "Say he died while being processed. Do the country a favor."

"That would produce a hell of a stink. Besides, we have no proof."

Mudgett flourished the protocol excitedly.

"That's not proof to anyone but a haemotologist."

"But Carson, the man's a saboteur!" Mudgett shouted. "Nobody but an Asiatic could have a typing pattern like this! And he's no melting-pot product, either – he's a classical mixture, very probably a Georgian. And every move he's made since we first heard of him has been aimed directly at us – aimed directly at tricking us into getting him into the machine!"

"I think so too," Carson said grimly. "I just hope the enemy hasn't many more agents as brilliant."

"One's enough," Mudgett said. "He's sure to be loaded to the last cc of his blood with catalyst poisons. Once the machine starts processing his serum, we're done for – it'll take us years to reprogram the computer, if it can be done at all. It's *got* to be stopped!"

"Stopped?" Carson said, astonished. "But it's already stopped. That's not what worries me. The machine stopped it fifty minutes ago."

"It can't have! How could it? It has no relevant data!"

"Sure it has." Carson leaned forward, took the cruelly chewed pencil away from Mudgett, and made a neat check beside one of the entries on the protocol. Mudgett stared at the checked item.

"Platelets Rh VI?" he mumbled. "But what's that got to do with . . . Oh. Oh, I see. That platelet type doesn't exist at all in our population now, does it? Never seen it before myself, at least."

"No," Carson said, grinning wolfishly. "It never was common in the West, and the pogrom of 1981 wiped it out. That's something the enemy couldn't know. But the machine knows it. As soon as it gives him the standard anti-IV desensitization shot, his platelets will begin to dissolve – and he'll be rejected for incipient thrombocytopenia." He laughed. "For his own protection! But —"

"But he's getting nitrous oxide in the machine, and he'll be held six hours under anesthesia anyhow – also for his own protection," Mudgett broke in. He was grinning back at Carson like an idiot. "When he comes out from under, he'll assume that he's been re-educated, and he'll beat it back to the enemy to report that he's poisoned our machine, so that they can be sure they'll beat us to the surface. And he'll go the fastest way: *overland.*"

"He will," Carson agreed. "Of course he'll go overland, and of course he'll die. But where does that leave us? We won't be able to conceal that he was treated here, if there's any sort of inquiry at all. And his death will make everything we do here look like a fraud. Instead of paying our Pied Piper – and great jumping Jehoshaphat, look at his name! They were rubbing our noses in it all the time! Nevertheless, we didn't pay the piper; we killed him. And 'platelets Rh VI' won't be an adequate excuse for the press, or for Hamelin's following."

"It doesn't worry me," Mudgett rumbled. "Who'll know? He won't die in our labs. He'll leave here hale and hearty. He won't die until he makes a break for the surface. After that we can compose a fine obituary for the press. Heroic government official, on the highest policy level – couldn't wait to lead his followers to the surface – died of being too much in a hurry – Re-Ed Project sorrowfully reminds everyone that no technique is foolproof . . ."

Mudgett paused long enough to light a cigarette, which was a most singular action for a man who never smoked. "As a matter of fact, Carson," he said, "it's a natural."

Carson considered it. It seemed to hold up. And

27

'Hamelin' would have a death certificate as complex as he deserved – not officially, of course, but in the minds of everyone who knew the facts. His death, when it came, would be due directly to the thrombocytopenia which had caused the Re-Ed-machine to reject him – and thrombocytopenia is a disease of infants. *Unless ye become as little children* . . .

That was a fitting reason for rejection from the new kingdom of Earth: anemia of the newborn.

His pent breath went out of him in a long sigh. He hadn't been aware that he'd been holding it. "It's true," he said softly. "That's the time to pay the piper."

"When?" Mudget said.

"When?" Carson said, surprised. "Why, *before* he takes the children away."

Beep

Josef Faber lowered his newspaper slightly. Finding the girl on the park bench looking his way, he smiled the agonizingly embarrassed smile of the thoroughly married nobody caught bird-watching, and ducked back into the paper again.

He was reasonably certain that he looked the part of a middle-aged, steadily employed, harmless citizen enjoying a Sunday break in the bookkeeping and family routines. He was also quite certain, despite his official instructions, that it wouldn't make the slightest bit of difference if he didn't. These boy-meets-girl assignments always came off. Jo had never tackled a single one that had required him.

As a matter of fact, the newspaper, which he was supposed to be using only as a blind, interested him a good deal more than his job did. He had only barely begun to suspect the obvious ten years ago when the Service had snapped him up; now, after a decade as an agent, he was still fascinated to see how smoothly the really important situations came off. The *dangerous* situations – not boy-meets-girl.

This affair of the Black Horse Nebula, for instance. Some days ago the papers and the commentators had begun to mention reports of disturbances in that area, and Jo's practiced eye had picked up the mention. Something big was cooking.

Today it had boiled over – the Black Horse Nebula had suddenly spewed ships by the hundreds, a massed armada that must have taken more than a century of effort on the

29

part of a whole star cluster, a production drive conducted in the strictest and most fanatical kind of secrecy . . .

And, of course, the Service had been on the spot in plenty of time. With three times as many ships, disposed with mathematical precision so as to enfilade the entire armada the moment it broke from the nebula. The battle had been a massacre, the attack smashed before the average citizen could even begin to figure out what it had been aimed at – and good had triumphed over evil once more.

Of course.

Furtive scuffings on the gravel drew his attention briefly. He looked at his watch, which said 14:58:03. That was the time, according to his instructions, when boy had to meet girl.

He had been given the strictest kind of orders to let nothing interfere with this meeting – the orders always issued on boy-meets-girl assignments. But, as usual, he had nothing to do but observe. The meeting was coming off on the dot, without any prodding from Jo. They always did.

Of course.

With a sigh, he folded his newspaper, smiling again at the couple – yes, it was the right man, too – and moved away, as if reluctantly. He wondered what would happen were he to pull away the false mustache, pitch the newspaper on the grass, and bound away with a joyous whoop. He suspected that the course of history would not be deflected by even a second of arc, but he was not minded to try the experiment.

The park was pleasant. The twin suns warmed the path and the greenery without any of the blasting heat which they would bring to bear later in the summer. Randolph was altogether the most comfortable planet he had visited in years. A little backward, perhaps, but restful, too.

It was also slightly over a hundred light-years away from Earth. It would be interesting to know how Service headquarters on Earth could have known in advance that boy would meet girl at a certain spot on Randolph, precisely at 14:58:03.

Or how Service headquarters could have ambushed with micrometric precision a major interstellar fleet, with no more preparation than a few days' buildup in the newspapers and video could evidence.

The press was free, on Randolph as everywhere. It reported the news it got. Any emergency concentration of Service ships in the Black Horse area, or anywhere else, would have been noticed and reported on. The Service did not forbid such reports for 'security' reasons or for any other reasons. Yet there had been nothing to report but that (a) an armada of staggering size had erupted with no real warning from the Black Horse Nebula, and that (b) the Service had been ready.

By now, it was a commonplace that the Service was always ready. It had not had a defect or failure in well over two centuries. It had not even had a fiasco, the alarming-sounding technical word by which it referred to the possibility that a boy-meets-girl assignment might not come off.

Jo hailed a hopper. Once inside he stripped himself of the mustache, the bald spot, the forehead creases – all the make-up which had given him his mask of friendly innocuousness.

The hoppy watched the whole process in the rear-view mirror. Jo glanced up and met his eyes.

"Pardon me, mister, but I figured you didn't care if I saw you. You must be a Service man."

"That's right. Take me to Service HQ, will you?"

"Sure enough." The hoppy gunned his machine. It rose smoothly to the express level. "First time I ever got close to a Service man. Didn't hardly believe it at first when I saw you taking your face off. You sure looked different."

"Have to, sometimes," Jo said, preoccupied.

"I'll bet. No wonder you know all about everything before it breaks. You must have a thousand faces each, your own

31

mother wouldn't know you, eh? Don't you care if I know about your snooping around in disguise?"

Jo grinned. The grin created a tiny pulling sensation across one curve of his cheek, just next to his nose. He stripped away the overlooked bit of tissue and examined it critically.

"Of course not. Disguise is an elementary part of Service work. Anyone could guess that. We don't use it often, as a matter of fact – only on very simple assignments."

"Oh." The hoppy sounded slightly disappointed, as melodrama faded. He drove silently for about a minute. Then, speculatively: "Sometimes I think the Service must have time-travel, the things they pull . . . Well, here you are. Good luck, mister."

"Thanks."

Jo went directly to Krasna's office. Krasna was a Randolpher. Earth-trained, and answerable to the Earth office, but otherwise pretty much on his own. His heavy, muscular face wore the same expression of serene confidence that was characteristic of Service officials everywhere – even some that, technically speaking, had no faces to wear it.

"Boy meets girl," Jo said briefly. "On the nose and on the spot."

"Good work, Jo. Cigarette?" Krasna pushed the box across his desk.

"Nope, not now. Like to talk to you, if you've got time."

Krasna pushed a button, and a toadstoollike chair rose out of the floor behind Jo. "What's on your mind?"

"Well," Jo said carefully. "I'm wondering why you patted me on the back just now for not doing a job."

"You did a job."

"I did not," Jo said flatly. "Boy would have met girl, whether I'd been here on Randolph or back on Earth. The course of true love always runs smooth. It has in all my boy-meets-girl cases, and it has in the boy-meets-girl cases of every other agent with whom I've compared notes."

"Well, good," Krasna said, smiling. "That's the way we like to have it run. And that's the way we expect it to run. But, Jo, we like to have somebody on the spot, somebody with a reputation for resourcefulness, just in case there's a snag. There almost never is, as you've observed. But – if there were?"

Jo snorted. "If what you're trying to do is to establish preconditions for the future, any interference by a Service agent would throw the eventual result farther *off* the track. I know that much about probability."

"And what makes you think that we're trying to set up the future?"

"It's obvious even to the hoppies on your own planet; the one that brought me here told me he thought the Service had time-travel. It's especially obvious to all the individuals and governments and entire populations that the Service has bailed out of serious messes for centuries, with never a single failure." Jo shrugged. "A man can be asked to safeguard only a small number of boy-meets-girl cases before he realizes, as an agent, that what the Service is safeguarding is the future children of those meetings. Ergo – the Service *knows* what those children are to be like, and has reason to want their future existence guaranteed. What other conclusion is possible?"

Krasna took out a cigarette and lit it deliberately; it was obvious that he was using the maneuver to cloak his response.

"None," he admitted at last. "We have some foreknowledge, of course. We couldn't have made our reputation with espionage alone. But we have obvious other advantages: genetics, for instance, and operations research, the theory of games, the Dirac transmitter – it's quite an arsenal, and of course there's a good deal of prediction involved in all those things."

"I see that," Jo said. He shifted in his chair, formulating all he wanted to say. He changed his mind about the cigarette and helped himself to one. "But these things don't add up to infallibility – and that's a qualitative difference, Kras. Take this affair of the Black Horse armada. The moment the armada appeared, we'll assume, Earth heard about it by Dirac, and started to assemble a counterarmada. But it takes *finite time* to bring together a concentration of ships and men, even if your message system is instantaneous.

"The Service's counterarmada was *already on hand*. It had been building there for so long and with so little fuss that nobody even noticed it concentrating until a day or so before the battle. Then planets in the area began to sit up and take notice, and be uneasy about what was going to break. But not very uneasy; the Service always wins – that's been a statistical fact for centuries. *Centuries*, Kras. Good Lord, it takes almost as long as that, in straight preparation, to pull some of the tricks we've pulled! The Dirac gives us an advantage of ten to twenty-five years in really extreme cases out on the rim of the Galaxy, but no more than that."

He realized that he had been fuming away on the cigarette until the roof of his mouth was scorched, and snubbed it out angrily. "That's a very different thing," he said, "than knowing in a general way how an enemy is likely to behave, or what kind of children the Mendelian laws say a given couple should have. It means that we've some way of reading the future in minute detail. That's in flat contradiction to everything I've been taught about probability, but I have to believe what I see."

Krasna laughed. "That's a very able presentation," he said. He seemed genuinely pleased. "I think you'll remember that you were first impressed into the Service when you began to wonder why the news was always good. Fewer and fewer people wonder about that nowadays; it's become a part of their expected environment." He stood up and ran a hand through his hair. "Now you've carried yourself through the next stage. Congratulations, Jo. You've just been promoted!"

"I have?" Jo said incredulously. "I came in here with the notion that I might get myself fired."

34

"No. Come around to this side of the desk, Jo, and I'll play you a little history." Krasna unfolded the desk-top to expose a small visor screen. Obediently Jo rose and went around the desk to where he could see the blank surface. "I had a standard indoctrination tape sent up to me a week ago, in the expectation that you'd be ready to see it. Watch."

Krasna touched the board. A small dot of light appeared in the center of the screen and went out again. At the same time, there was a small *beep* of sound. Then the tape began to unroll and a picture clarified on the screen.

"As you suspected," Krasna said conversationally, "the Service is infallible. How it got that way is a story that started several centuries back."

II

Dana Lje – her father had been a Hollander, her mother born in the Celebes – sat down in the chair which Captain Robin Weinbaum had indicated, crossed her legs, and waited, her blue-black hair shining under the lights.

Weinbaum eyed her quizzically. The conqueror Resident who had given the girl her entirely European name had been paid in kind, for his daughter's beauty had nothing fair and Dutch about it. To the eye of the beholder, Dana Lje seemed a particularly delicate virgin of Bali, despite her Western name, clothing and assurance. The combination had already proven piquant for the millions who watched her television column, and Weinbaum found it no less charming at first hand.

"As one of your most recent victims," he said, "I'm not sure that I'm honored, Miss Lje. A few of my wounds are still bleeding. But I am a good deal puzzled as to why you're visiting me now. Aren't you afraid that I'll bite back?"

"I had no intention of attacking you personally, and I don't think I did," the video columnist said seriously. "It was just pretty plain that our intelligence had slipped badly

35

in the Erskine affair. It was my job to say so. Obviously you were going to get hurt, since you're head of the bureau – but there was no malice in it."

"Cold comfort," Weinbaum said dryly. "But thank you, nevertheless."

The Eurasian girl shrugged. "That isn't what I came here about, anyway. Tell me, Captain Weinbaum – have you ever heard of an outfit calling itself Interstellar Information?"

Weinbaum shook his head. "Sounds like a skip-tracing firm. Not an easy business, these days."

"That's just what I thought when I first saw their letterhead," Dana said. "But the letter under it wasn't one that a private-eye outfit would write. Let me read part of it to you."

Her slim fingers burrowed in her inside jacket pocket and emerged again with a single sheet of paper. It was plain typewriter bond, Weinbaum noted automatically: she had brought only a copy with her, and had left the original of the letter at home. The copy, then, would be incomplete – probably seriously.

"It goes like this: 'Dear Miss Lje: As a syndicated video commentator with a wide audience and heavy responsibilities, you need the best sources of information available. We would like you to test our service, free of charge, in the hope of proving to you that it is superior to any other source of news on Earth. Therefore, we offer below several predictions concerning events to come in the Hercules and the so-called "Three Ghosts" areas. If these predictions are fulfilled 100 per cent – no less – we ask that you take us on as your correspondents for those areas, at rates to be agreed upon later. If the predictions are wrong in *any* respect, you need not consider us further.'"

"H'm," Weinbaum said slowly. "They're confident cusses – and that's an odd juxtaposition. The Three Ghosts make up only a little solar system, while the Hercules area could include the entire star cluster – or maybe even the whole constellation, which is a hell of a lot of sky. This outfit

36

seems to be trying to tell you that it has thousands of field correspondents of its own, maybe as many as the government itself. If so, I'll guarantee that they're bragging."

"That may well be so. But before you make up your mind, let me read you one of the two predictions." The letter rustled in Dana Lje's hand. "'At 03:16:10, on Year Day, 2090, the Hess-type interstellar liner *Brindisi* will be attacked in the neighborhood of the Three Ghosts system by four —'"

Weinbaum sat bolt upright in his swivel chair. "Let me see that letter!" he said, his voice harsh with repressed alarm.

"In a moment," the girl said, adjusting her skirt composedly. "Evidently I was right in riding my hunch. Let me go on reading: ' – by four heavily armed vessels flying the lights of the navy of Hammersmith II. The position of the liner at that time will be at coded co-ordinates 88-A-theta-88-aleph-D and-per-se-and. It will —'"

"Miss Lje," Weinbaum said. "I'm sorry to interrupt you again, but what you've said already would justify me in jailing you at once, no matter how loudly your sponsors might scream. I don't know about this Interstellar Information outfit, or whether or not you did receive any such letter as the one you pretend to be quoting. But I can tell you that you've shown yourself to be in possession of information that only yours truly and four other men are supposed to know. It's already too late to tell you that everything you say may be held against you; all I can say now is, it's high time you clammed up!"

"I thought so," she said, apparently not disturbed in the least. "Then that liner *is* scheduled to hit those co-ordinates, and the coded time co-ordinate corresponds with the predicted Universal Time. Is it also true that the *Brindisi* will be carrying a top-secret communication device?"

"Are you deliberately trying to make me imprison you?" Weinbaum said, gritting his teeth. "Or is this just a stunt, designed to show me that my own bureau is full of leaks?"

"It could turn into that," Dana admitted. "But it hasn't, yet. Robin, I've been as honest with you as I'm able to be. You've had nothing but square deals from me up to now. I wouldn't yellow-screen you, and you know it. If this unknown outfit has this information, it might easily have gotten it from where it hints that it got it, from the field."

"Impossible."

"Why?"

"Because the information in question hasn't even reached my *own* agents in the field yet – it couldn't possibly have leaked as far as Hammersmith II or anywhere else, let alone to the Three Ghosts system! Letters have to be carried on ships, you know that. If I were to send orders by ultrawave to my Three Ghosts agent, he'd have to wait three hundred and twenty-four years to get them. By ship, he can get them in a little over two months. These particular orders have only been under way to him five days. Even if somebody has read them on board the ship that's carrying them, they couldn't possibly be sent on to the Three Ghosts any faster than they're traveling now."

Dana nodded her dark head. "All right. Then what are we left with but a leak in your headquarters here?"

"What, indeed," Weinbaum said grimly. "You'd better tell me who signed this letter of yours."

"The signature is J. Shelby Stevens."

Weinbaum switched on the intercom. "Margaret, look in the business register for an outfit called Interstellar Information and find out who owns it."

Dana Lje said, "Aren't you interested in the rest of the prediction?"

"You bet I am. Does it tell you the name of this communications device?"

"Yes," Dana said.

"What is it?"

"The Dirac communicator."

Weinbaum groaned and turned on the intercom again.

38

"Margaret, send in Dr. Wald. Tell him to drop everything and gallop. Any luck with the other thing?"

"Yes, sir," the intercom said. "It's a one-man outfit, wholly owned by a J. Shelby Stevens, in Rico City. It was first registered this year."

"Arrest him, on suspicion of espionage."

The door swung open and Dr. Wald came in, all six and a half feet of him. He was extremely blond, and looked awkward, gentle, and not very intelligent.

"Thor, this young lady is our press nemesis, Dana Lje. Dana, Dr. Wald is the inventor of the Dirac communicator, about which you have so damnably much information."

"It's out *already?*" Dr. Wald said, scanning the girl with grave deliberation.

"It is, and lots more – *lots* more. Dana, you're a good girl at heart, and for some reason I trust you, stupid though it is to trust anybody in this job. I should detain you until Year Day, videocasts or no videocasts. Instead, I'm just going to ask you to sit on what you've got, and I'm going to explain why."

"Shoot."

"I've already mentioned how slow communication is between star and star. We have to carry all our letters on ships, just as we did locally before the invention of the telegraph. The overdrive lets us beat the speed of light, but not by much of a margin over really long distances. Do you understand that?"

"Certainly," Dana said. She appeared a bit nettled, and Weinbaum decided to give her the full dose at a more rapid pace. After all, she could be assumed to be better informed than the average layman.

"What we've needed for a long time, then," he said, "is some virtually instantaneous method of getting a message from somewhere to anywhere. Any time lag, no matter how small it seems at first, has a way of becoming major as longer and longer distances are involved. Sooner or later we must have this instantaneous method, or we won't be able to get

39

messages from one system to another fast enough to hold our jurisdiction over outlying regions of space."

"Wait a minute," Dana said. "I'd always understood that ultrawave is faster than light."

"Effectively it is; physically it isn't. You don't understand that?"

She shook her dark head.

"In a nutshell," Weinbaum said, "ultrawave is radiation, and all radiation in free space is limited to the speed of light. The way we hype up ultrawave is to use an old application of wave-guide theory, whereby the real transmission of energy is at light speed, but an imaginary thing called 'phase velocity' is going faster. But the gain in speed of transmission isn't large – by ultrawave, for instance, we get a message to Alpha Centauri in one year instead of nearly four. Over long distances, that's not nearly enough extra speed."

"Can't it be speeded further?" she said, frowning.

"No. Think of the ultrawave beam between here and Centaurus III as a caterpillar. The caterpillar himself is moving quite slowly, just at the speed of light. But the pulses which pass along his body are going forward faster than he is – and if you've ever watched a caterpillar, you'll know that that's true. But there's a physical limit to the number of pulses you can travel along that caterpillar, and we've already reached that limit. We've taken phase velocity as far as it will go.

"That's why we need something faster. For a long time our relativity theories discouraged hope of anything faster – even the high-phase velocity of a guided wave didn't contradict those theories; it just found a limited, mathematically imaginary loophole in them. But when Thor here began looking into the question of the velocity of propagation of a Dirac pulse, he found the answer. The communicator he developed does seem to act over long distances, *any* distance, instantaneously – and it may wind up knocking relativity into a cocked hat."

The girl's face was a study in stunned realization. "I'm not sure I've taken in all the technical angles," she said. "But if I'd had any notion of the political dynamite in this thing —"

"– you'd have kept out of my office," Weinbaum said grimly. "A good thing you didn't. The *Brindisi* is carrying a model of the Dirac communicator out to the periphery for a final test; the ship is supposed to get in touch with me from out there at a given Earth time, which we've calculated very elaborately to account for the residual Lorentz and Milne transformations involved in overdrive flight, and for a lot of other time phenomena that wouldn't mean anything at all to you.

"If that signal arrives here at the given Earth time, then – aside from the havoc it will create among the theoretical physicists whom we decide to let in on it – we will really have our instant communicator, and can include all of occupied space in the same time zone. And we'll have a terrific advantage over any lawbreaker who has to resort to ultrawave locally and to letters carried by ships over the long haul."

"Not," Dr. Wald said sourly, "if it's already leaked out."

"It remains to be seen how much of it has leaked," Weinbaum said. "The principle is rather esoteric, Thor, and the name of the thing alone wouldn't mean much even to a trained scientist. I gather that Dana's mysterious informant didn't go into technical details . . . or did he?"

"No," Dana said.

"Tell the truth, Dana. I know that you're suppressing some of that letter."

The girl started slightly. "All right – yes, I am. But nothing technical. There's another part of the prediction that lists the number and class of ships you will send to protect the *Brindisi* – the prediction says they'll be sufficient, by the way – and I'm keeping that to myself, to see whether or

41

not it comes true along with the rest. If it does, I think I've hired myself a correspondent."

"If it does," Weinbaum said, "you've hired yourself a jailbird. Let's see how much mind reading J. Whatsit Stevens can do from the subcellar of Fort Yaphank."

III

Weinbaum let himself into Steven's cell, locking the door behind him and passing the keys out to the guard. He sat down heavily on the nearest stool.

Stevens smiled the weak benevolent smile of the very old, and laid his book aside on the bunk. The book, Weinbaum knew – since his office had cleared it – was only a volume of pleasant, harmless lyrics by a New Dynasty poet named Nims.

"Were our predictions correct, Captain?" Stevens said. His voice was high and musical, rather like that of a boy soprano.

Weinbaum nodded. "You still won't tell us how you did it?"

"But I already have," Stevens protested. "Our intelligence network is the best in the Universe, Captain. It is superior even to your own excellent organization, as events have shown."

"Its results are superior, that I'll grant," Weinbaum said glumly. "If Dana Lje had thrown your letter down her disposal chute, we would have lost the *Brindisi* and our Dirac transmitter both. Incidentally, did your original letter predict accurately the number of ships we would send?"

Stevens nodded pleasantly, his neatly trimmed white beard thrusting forward slightly as he smiled.

"I was afraid so," Weinbaum leaned forward. "Do you have the Dirac transmitter, Stevens?"

"Of course, Captain. How else could my correspondents report to me with the efficiency you have observed?"

"Then why don't our receivers pick up the broadcasts of

42

your agents? Dr. Wald says it's inherent in the principle that Dirac 'casts are picked up by *all* instruments tuned to receive them, bar none. And at this stage of the game there are so few such broadcasts being made that we'd be almost certain to detect any that weren't coming from our own operatives."

"I decline to answer that question, if you'll excuse the impoliteness," Stevens said, his voice quavering slightly. "I am an old man, Captain, and this intelligence agency is my sole source of income. If I told you how we operated, we would no longer have any advantage over your own service, except for the limited freedom from secrecy which we have. I have been assured by competent lawyers that I have every right to operate a private investigation bureau, properly licensed, upon any scale that I may choose, and that I have the right to keep my methods secret, as the so-called 'intellectual assets' of my firm. If you wish to use our services, well and good. We will provide them, with absolute guarantees on all information we furnish you, for an appropriate fee. But our methods are our own property."

Robin Weinbaum smiled twistedly. "I'm not a naïve man, Mr. Stevens," he said. "My service is hard on naïveté. You know as well as I do that the government can't allow you to operate on a free-lance basis, supplying top-secret information to anyone who can pay the price, or even free of charge to video columnists on a 'test' basis, even though you arrive at every jot of that information independently of espionage – which I still haven't entirely ruled out, by the way. If you can duplicate this *Brindisi* performance at will, we will have to have your services exclusively. In short, you become a hired civilian arm of my own bureau."

"Quite," Stevens said, returning the smile in a fatherly way. "We anticipated that, of course. However, we have contracts with other governments to consider; Erskine, in particular. If we are to work exclusively for Earth, necessarily our price will include compensation for renouncing our other accounts."

"Why should it? Patriotic public servants work for their government at a loss, if they can't work for it any other way."

"I am quite aware of that. I am quite prepared to renounce my other interests. But I do require to be paid."

"How much?" Weinbaum said, suddenly aware that his fists were clenched so tightly that they hurt.

Stevens appeared to consider, nodding his flowery white poll in senile deliberation. "My associates would have to be consulted. Tentatively, however, a sum equal to the present appropriation of your bureau would do, pending further negotiations."

Weinbaum shot to his feet, eyes wide. "You old buccaneer! You know damned well that I can't spend my entire appropriation on a single civilian service! Did it ever occur to you that most of the civilian outfits working for us are on cost-plus contracts, and that our civilian executives are being paid just a credit a year, by their own choice? You're demanding nearly two thousand credits an hour from your own government, and claiming the legal protection that the government affords you at the same time, in order to let those fanatics on Erskine run up a higher bid!"

"The price is not unreasonable," Stevens said. "The service is worth the price."

"That's where you're wrong! We have the discoverer of the machine working for us. For less than half the sum you're asking, we can find the application of the device that you're trading on – of that you can be damned sure."

"A dangerous gamble, Captain."

"Perhaps. We'll soon see!" Weinbaum glared at the placid face. "I'm forced to tell you that you're a free man, Mr. Stevens. We've been unable to show that you came by your information by any illegal method. You had classified facts in your possession, but no classified documents, and it's your privilege as a citizen to make guesses, no matter how educated.

"But we'll catch up with you sooner or later. Had you

been reasonable, you might have found yourself in a very good position with us, your income as assured as any political income can be, and your person respected to the hilt. Now, however, you're subject to censorship – you have no idea how humiliating that can be, but I'm going to see to it that you find out. There'll be no more newsbeats for Dana Lje, or for anyone else. I want to see every word of copy that you file with any client outside the bureau. Every word that is of use to me will be used, and you'll be paid the statutory one cent a word for it – the same rate that the FBI pays for anonymous gossip. Everything I don't find useful will be killed without clearance. Eventually we'll have the modification of the Dirac that you're using, and when that happens, you'll be so flat broke that a pancake with a harelip could spit right over you."

Weinbaum paused for a moment, astonished at his own fury.

Stevens's clarinetlike voice began to sound in the windowless cavity. "Captain, I have no doubt that you can do this to me, at least incompletely. But it will prove fruitless. I will give you a prediction, at no charge. It is guaranteed, as are all our predictions. It is this: *You will never find that modification*. Eventually, I will give it to you, on my own terms, but you will never find it for yourself, nor will you force it out of me. In the meantime, not a word of copy will be filed with you; for, despite the fact that you are an arm of the government, I can well afford to wait you out."

"Bluster," Weinbaum said.

"Fact. Yours is the bluster – loud talk based on nothing more than a hope. I, however, *know* whereof I speak . . . But let us conclude this discussion. It serves no purpose; you will need to see my points made the hard way. Thank you for giving me my freedom. We will talk again under different circumstances on – let me see; ah, yes, on June 9 of the year 2091. That year is, I believe, almost upon us."

Stevens picked up his book again, nodding at Weinbaum,

45

his expression harmless and kindly, his hands showing the marked tremor of *paralysis agitans*. Weinbaum moved helplessly to the door and flagged the turnkey. As the bars closed behind him, Stevens's voice called out: "Oh, yes; and a Happy New Year, Captain."

Weinbaum blasted his way back into his own office, at least twice as mad as the proverbial nest of hornets, and at the same time rather dismally aware of his own probable future. If Stevens's second prediction turned out to be as phenomenally accurate as his first had been, Capt. Robin Weinbaum would soon be peddling a natty set of secondhand uniforms.

He glared down at Margaret Soames, his receptionist. She glared right back; she had known him too long to be intimidated.

"Anything?" he said.

"Dr. Wald's waiting for you in your office. There are some field reports, and a couple of Diracs on your private tape. Any luck with the old codger?"

"That," he said crushingly, "is Top Secret."

"Poof. That means that nobody still knows the answer but J. Shelby Stevens."

He collapsed suddenly. "You're so right. That's just what it does mean. But we'll bust him wide open sooner or later. We've *got* to."

"You'll do it," Margaret said. "Anything else for me?"

"No. Tip off the clerical staff that there's a half holiday today, then go take in a stereo or a steak or something yourself. Dr. Wald and I have a few private wires to pull . . . and unless I'm sadly mistaken, a private bottle of aquavit to empty."

"Right," the receptionist said. "Tie one on for me, Chief. I understand that beer is the best chaser for aquavit – I'll have some sent up."

"If you should return after I am suitably squiffed," Weinbaum said, feeling a little better already, "I will kiss you for your thoughtfulness. *That* should keep you at your stereo at least twice through the third feature."

As he went on through the door of his own office, she said demurely behind him, "It certainly should."

As soon as the door closed, however, his mood became abruptly almost as black as before. Despite his comparative youth – he was now only fifty-five – he had been in the service a long time, and he needed no one to tell him the possible consequences which might flow from possession by a private citizen of the Dirac communicator. If there was ever to be a Federation of Man in the Galaxy, it was within the power of J. Shelby Stevens to ruin it before it had fairly gotten started. And there seemed to be nothing at all that could be done about it.

"Hello, Thor," he said glumly. "Pass the bottle."

"Hello, Robin. I gather things went badly. Tell me about it."

Briefly, Weinbaum told him. "And the worst of it," he finished, "is that Stevens himself predicts that we won't find the application of the Dirac that he's using, and that eventually we'll have to buy it at his price. Somehow I believe him – but I can't see how it's possible. If I were to tell Congress that I was going to spend my entire appropriation for a single civilian service, I'd be out on my ear within the next three sessions."

"Perhaps that isn't his real price," the scientist suggested. "If he wants to barter, he'd naturally begin with a demand miles above what he actually wants."

"Sure, sure . . . but frankly, Thor, I'd hate to give the old reprobate even a single credit if I could get out of it." Weinbaum sighed. "Well, let's see what's come in from the field."

Thor Wald moved silently away from Weinbaum's desk while the officer unfolded it and set up the Dirac screen. Stacked neatly next to the ultraphone – a device Weinbaum had been thinking of, only a few days ago, as permanently outmoded – were the tapes Margaret had mentioned. He fed the first one into the Dirac and turned the main toggle to the position labeled START.

Immediately the whole screen went pure white and the audio speakers emitted an almost instantly end-stopped blare of sound – a *beep* which, as Weinbaum already knew, made up a continuous spectrum from about 30 cycles per second to well above 18,000 cps. Then both the light and noise were gone as if they had never been, and were replaced by the familiar face and voice of Weinbaum's local ops chief in Rico City.

"There's nothing unusual in the way of transmitters in Stevens's offices here," the operative said without preamble. "And there isn't any local Interstellar Information staff, except for one stenographer, and she's as dumb as they come. About all we could get from her is that Stevens is 'such a sweet old man.' No possibility that she's faking it; she's genuinely stupid, the kind that thinks Betelgeuse is something Indians use to darken their skins. We looked for some sort of list or code table that would give us a line on Stevens's field staff, but that was another dead end. Now we're maintaining a twenty-four-hour Dinwiddie watch on the place from a joint across the street. Orders?"

Weinbaum dictated to the blank stretch of tape which followed: "Margaret, next time you send any Dirac tapes in here, cut that damnable *beep* off them first. Tell the boys in Rico City that Stevens has been released, and that I'm proceeding for an Order In Security to tap his ultraphone and his local lines – this is one case where I'm sure we can persuade the court that tapping's necessary. Also – and be damned sure you code this – tell them to proceed with the tap immediately and to maintain it regardless of whether or not the court O.K.s it. I'll thumbprint a Full Responsibility Confession for them. We can't afford to play pat-a-cake with Stevens – the potential is just too damned big. And oh, yes, Margaret, send the message by carrier, and send out general orders to everybody concerned not to use the Dirac again except when distance and time rule every other medium out. Stevens has already admitted that he can receive Dirac 'casts."

He put down the mike and stared morosely for a moment at the beautiful Eridanean scrollwood of his desktop. Wald coughed inquiringly and retrieved the aquavit.

"Excuse me, Robin," he said, "but I should think that would work both ways."

"So should I. And yet the fact is that we've never picked up so much as a whisper from either Stevens or his agents. I can't think of any way that could be pulled, but evidently it can."

"Well, let's rethink the problem, and see what we get," Wald said. "I didn't want to say so in front of the young lady, for obvious reasons – I mean Miss Lje, of course, not Margaret – but the truth is that the Dirac is essentially a simple mechanism in principle. I seriously doubt that there's any way to transmit a message from it which can't be detected – and an examination of the theory with that proviso in mind might give us something new."

"What proviso?" Weinbaum said. Thor Wald left him behind rather often these days.

"Why, that a Dirac transmission doesn't *necessarily* go to all communicators capable of receiving it. If that's true, then the reasons why it is true should emerge from the theory."

"I see. O.K., proceed on that line. I've been looking at Stevens's dossier while you were talking, and it's all an absolute desert. Prior to the opening of the office in Rico City, there's no dope whatever on J. Shelby Stevens. The man as good as rubbed my nose in the fact that he's using a pseud when I first talked to him. I asked him what the 'J' in his name stood for, and he said, 'Oh, let's make it Jerome.' But who the man behind the pseud *is* . . ."

"Is it possible that he's using his own initials?"

"No," Weinbaum said. "Only the dumbest ever do that, or transpose syllables, or retain any connection at all with their real names. Those are the people who are in

49

serious emotional trouble, people who drive themselves into anonymity, but leave clues strewn all around the landscape – those clues are really a cry for help, for discovery. Of course we're working on that angle – we can't neglect anything – but J. Shelby Stevens isn't that kind of case, I'm sure." Weinbaum stood up abruptly. "O.K., Thor – what's first on your technical program?"

"Well . . . I suppose we'll have to start with checking the frequencies we use. We're going on Dirac's assumption – and it works very well, and always has – that a positron in motion through a crystal lattice is accompanied by de Broglie waves which are transforms of the waves of an electron in motion somewhere else in the Universe. Thus if we control the frequency and path of the positron, we control the placement of the electron – we cause it to appear, so to speak, in the circuits of a communicator somewhere else. After that, reception is just a matter of amplifying the bursts and reading the signal."

Wald scowled and shook his blond head. "If Stevens is getting out messages which we don't pick up, my first assumption would be that he's worked out a fine-tuning circuit that's more delicate than ours, and is more or less sneaking his messages under ours. The only way that could be done, as far as I can see at the moment, is by something really fantastic in the way of exact frequency control of his positron gun. If so, the logical step for us is to go back to the beginning of our tests and rerun our diffractions to see if we can refine our measurements of positron frequencies."

The scientist looked so inexpressibly gloomy as he offered this conclusion that a pall of hopelessness settled over Weinbaum in sheer sympathy. "You don't look as if you expected that to uncover anything new."

"I don't. You see, Robin, things are different in physics now than they used to be in the twentieth century. In those days, it was always presupposed that physics was limitless – the classic statement was made by Weyl, who said that 'It is the nature of a real thing to be inexhaustible in

50

content.' We know now that that's not so, except in a remote, associational sort of way. Nowadays, physics is a defined and self-limited science; its scope is still prodigious, but we can no longer think of it as endless.

"This is better established in particle physics than in any other branch of the science. Half of the trouble physicists of the last century had with Euclidean geometry – and hence the reason why they evolved so many recomplicated theories of relativity – is that it's a geometry of lines, and thus can be subdivided infinitely. When Cantor proved that there really is an infinity, at least mathematically speaking, that seemed to clinch the case for the possibility of a really infinite physical universe, too."

Wald's eyes grew vague, and he paused to gulp down a slug of the licorice-flavored aquavit which would have made Weinbaum's every hair stand on end.

"I remember," Wald said, "the man who taught me theory of sets at Princeton, many years ago. He used to say: 'Cantor teaches us that there are many kinds of infinities. *There* was a crazy old man!'"

Weinbaum rescued the bottle hastily. "So go on, Thor."

"Oh." Wald blinked. "Yes. Well, what we know now is that the geometry which applies to ultimate particles, like the positron, isn't Euclidean at all. It's Pythagorean – a geometry of points, not lines. Once you've measured one of those points, and it doesn't matter what kind of quantity you're measuring, you're down as far as you can go. At that point, the Universe becomes discontinuous, and no further refinement is possible.

"And I'd say that our positron-frequency measurements have already gotten that far down. There isn't another element in the Universe denser than plutonium, yet we get the same frequency values by diffraction through plutonium crystals that we get through osmium crystals – there's not the slightest difference. If J. Shelby Stevens is operating in terms of fractions of those values, then he's doing what an organist would call 'playing in the cracks' –

which is certainly something you can *think* about doing, but something that's in actuality impossible to do. *Hoop*."

"Hoop?" Weinbaum said.

"Sorry. A hiccup only."

"Oh. Well, maybe Stevens has rebuilt the organ?"

"If he has rebuilt the metrical frame of the Universe to accommodate a private skip-tracing firm," Wald said firmly, "I for one see no reason why we can't counter-check him – *hoop* – by declaring the whole cosmos null and void."

"All right, all right," Weinbaum said, grinning. "I didn't mean to push your analogy right over the edge – I was just asking. But let's get to work on it anyhow. We can't just sit here and let Stevens get away with it. If this frequency angle turns out to be as hopeless as it seems, we'll try something else."

Wald eyed the aquavit bottle owlishly. "It's a very pretty problem," he said. "Have I ever sung you the song we have in Sweden called 'Nat-og-Dag?'"

"*Hoop*," Weinbaum said to his own surprise, in a high falsetto. "Excuse me. No. Let's hear it."

The computer occupied an entire floor of the Security building, its seemingly identical banks laid out side by side on the floor along an advanced pathological state of Peano's 'space-filling curve.' At the current business end of the line was a master control board with a large television screen at its center, at which Dr. Wald was stationed, with Weinbaum looking, silently but anxiously, over his shoulder.

The screen itself showed a pattern which, except that it was drawn in green light against a dark gray background, strongly resembled the grain in a piece of highly polished mahogany. Photographs of similar patterns were stacked on a small table to Dr. Wald's right; several had spilled over onto the floor.

"Well, there it is," Wald sighed at length. "And I won't struggle to keep myself from saying 'I told you so.' What

52

you've had me do here, Robin, is to reconfirm about half the basic postulates of particle physics – which is why it took so long, even though it was the first project we started." He snapped off the screen. "There are no cracks for J. Shelby to play in. That's definite."

"If you'd said 'That's flat,' you would have made a joke," Weinbaum said sourly. "Look . . . isn't there still a chance of error? If not on your part, Thor, then in the computer? After all, it's set up to work only with the unit charges of modern physics; mightn't we have to disconnect the banks that contain that bias before the machine will follow the fractional-charge instructions we give it?"

"'Disconnect,' he says," Wald groaned, mopping his brow reflectively. "The bias exists everywhere in the machine, my friend, because it functions everywhere on those same unit charges. It wasn't a matter of subtracting banks; we had to add one with a bias all its own, to countercorrect the corrections the computer would otherwise apply to the instructions. The technicians thought I was crazy. Now, five months later, I've proved it."

Weinbaum grinned in spite of himself. "What about the other projects?"

"All done – some time back, as a matter of fact. The staff and I checked every single Dirac tape we've received since you released J. Shelby from Yaphank, for any sign of intermodulation, marginal signals, or anything else of the kind. There's nothing, Robin, absolutely nothing. That's our net result, all around."

"Which leaves us just where we started," Weinbaum said. "All the monitoring projects came to the same dead end; I strongly suspect that Stevens hasn't risked any further calls from his home office to his field staff, even though he seemed confident that we'd never intercept such calls – as we haven't. Even our local wire tapping hasn't turned up anything but calls by Stevens's secretary, making appointments for him with various clients, actual and potential. Any information he's selling these days he's passing on in person – and not in his office, either, because we've got bugs planted all over that and haven't heard a thing."

"That must limit his range of operation enormously," Wald objected.

Weinbaum nodded. "Without a doubt – but he shows no signs of being bothered by it. He can't have sent any tips to Erskine recently, for instance, because our last tangle with that crew came out very well for us, even though we had to use the Dirac to send the orders to our squadron out there. If he overheard us, he didn't even try to pass the word. Just as he said, he's sweating us out — " Weinbaum paused. "Wait a minute, here comes Margaret. And by the length of her stride, I'd say she's got something particularly nasty on her mind."

"You bet I do," Margaret Soames said vindictively. "And it'll blow plenty of lids around here, or I miss my guess. The I. D. squad has finally pinned down J. Shelby Stevens. They did it with the voice-comparator alone."

"How does that work?" Wald said interestedly.

"Blink microphone," Weinbaum said impatiently. "Isolates inflections on single, normally stressed syllables and matches them. Standard I. D. searching technique, on a case of this kind, but it takes so long that we usually get the quarry by other means before it pays off. Well, don't stand there like a dummy, Margaret. Who is he?"

"'He,'" Margaret said, "is your sweetheart of the video waves, Miss Dana Lje."

"They're crazy!" Wald said, staring at her.

Weinbaum came slowly out of his first shock of stunned disbelief. "No, Thor," he said finally. "No, it figures. If a woman is going to go in for disguises, there are always two she can assume outside her own sex: a young boy, and a very old man. And Dana's an actress; that's no news to us."

"But – but why did she do it, Robin?"

"That's what we're going to find out right now. So we wouldn't get the Dirac modification by ourselves, eh! Well, there are other ways of getting answers besides particle physics. Margaret, do you have a pick-up order out for that girl?"

"No," the receptionist said. "This is one chestnut I wanted to see you pull out for yourself. You give me the authority, and I send the order – not before."

"Spiteful child. Send it, then, and glory in my gritted teeth. Come on, Thor – let's put the nutcracker on this chestnut."

As they were leaving the computer floor, Weinbaum stopped suddenly in his tracks and began to mutter in an almost inaudible voice.

Wald said, "What's the matter, Robin?"

"Nothing. I keep being brought up short by those predictions. What's the date?"

"M'm . . . June 9. Why?"

"It's the exact date that 'Stevens' predicted we'd meet again, damn it! Something tells me that this isn't going to be as simple as it looks."

If Dana Lje had any idea of what she was in for – and considering the fact that she was 'J. Shelby Stevens' it had to be assumed that she did – the knowledge seemed not to make her at all fearful. She sat as composedly as ever before Weinbaum's desk, smoking her eternal cigarette, and waited, one dimpled knee pointed directly at the bridge of the officer's nose.

"Dana," Weinbaum said, "this time we're going to get all the answers, and we're not going to be gentle about it. Just in case you're not aware of the fact, there are certain laws relating to giving false information to a security officer, under which we could heave you in prison for a minimum of fifteen years. By application of the statutes on using communications to defraud, plus various local laws against transvestism, pseudonymity and so on, we could probably pile up enough additional short sentences to keep you in Yaphank until you really *do* grow a beard. So I'd advise you to open up."

"I have every intention of opening up," Dana said. "I know, practically word for word, how this interview is going to proceed, what information I'm going to give you, just when I'm going to give it to you – and what you're going to pay me for it. I knew all that many months ago. So there would be no point in my holding out on you."

"What you're saying, Miss Lje," Thor Wald said in a resigned voice, "is that the future is fixed, and that you can read it, in every essential detail."

"Quite right, Dr. Wald. Both those things are true."

There was a brief silence.

"All right," Weinbaum said grimly. "Talk."

"All right, Captain Weinbaum, pay me," Dana said calmly.

Weinbaum snorted.

"But I'm quite serious," she said. "You still don't know what I know about the Dirac communicator, I won't be forced to tell it, by threat of prison or by any other threat. You see, I know for a fact that you aren't going to send me to prison, or give me drugs, or do anything else of that kind. I know for a fact, instead, that you are going to pay me – so I'd be very foolish to say a word until you do. After all, it's quite a secret you're buying. Once I tell you what it is, you and the entire service will be able to read the future as I do, and then the information will be valueless to me."

Weinbaum was completely speechless for a moment. Finally he said, "Dana, you have a heart of purest brass, as well as a knee with an invisible gunsight on it. I say that I'm *not* going to give you my appropriation, regardless of what the future may or may not say about it. I'm not going to give it to you because the way my government – and yours – runs things makes such a price impossible. Or is that really your price?"

"It's my real price . . . but it's also an alternative. Call it my second choice. My first choice, which means the price

I'd settle for, comes in two parts: (a) to be taken into your service as a responsible officer; and, (b) to be married to Captain Robin Weinbaum."

Weinbaum sailed up out of his chair. He felt as though copper-colored flames a foot long were shooting out of each of his ears.

"Of all the — " he began. There his voice failed completely.

From behind him, where Wald was standing, came something like a large, Scandinavian-model guffaw being choked into insensibility.

Dana herself seemed to be smiling a little.

"You see," she said, "I don't point my best and most accurate knee at every man I meet."

Weinbaum sat down again, slowly and carefully. "Walk, do not run, to nearest exit," he said. "Women and childlike security officers first. Miss Lje, are you trying to sell me the notion that you went through this elaborate hanky-panky – beard and all – out of a burning passion for my dumpy and underpaid person?"

"Not entirely," Dana Lje said. "I want to be in the bureau, too, as I said. Let me confront you, though, Captain, with a fact of life that doesn't seem to have occurred to you at all. Do you accept as a fact that I can read the future in detail, and that that, to be possible at all, means that the future is fixed?"

"Since Thor seems able to accept it, I suppose I can too – provisionally."

"There's nothing provisional about it," Dana said firmly. "Now, when I first came upon this – uh, this gimmick – quite a while back, one of the first things that I found out was that I was going to go through the 'J. Shelby Stevens' masquerade, force myself onto the staff of the bureau, and marry you, Robin. At the time, I was both astonished and completely rebellious. I didn't want to be on the bureau staff; I liked my free-lance life as a video commentator. I didn't want to marry you, though I wouldn't have been

57

averse to living with you for a while – say a month or so. And above all, the masquerade struck me as ridiculous.

"But the facts kept staring me in the face. I *was* going to do all those things. There were no alternatives, no fanciful 'branches of time,' no decision-points that might be altered to make the future change. My future, like yours, Dr. Wald's, and everyone else's, was fixed. It didn't matter a snap whether or not I had a decent motive for what I was going to do; I was going to do it anyhow. Cause and effect, as I could see for myself, just don't exist. One event follows another because events are just as indestructible in space-time as matter and energy are.

"It was the bitterest of all pills. It will take me many years to swallow it completely, and you too. Dr. Wald will come around a little sooner, I think. At any rate, once I was intellectually convinced that all this was so, I had to protect my own sanity. I knew that I couldn't alter what I was going to do, but the least I could do to protect myself was to supply myself with motives. Or, in other words, just plain rationalizations. That much, it seems, we're free to do; the consciousness of the observer is just along for the ride through time, and can't alter events – but it can comment, explain, invent. That's fortunate, for none of us could stand going through motions which were truly free of what we think of as personal significance.

"So I supplied myself with the obvious motives. Since I was going to be married to you and couldn't get out of it, I set out to convince myself that I loved you. Now I do. Since I was going to join the bureau staff, I thought over all the advantages that it might have over video commentating, and found that they made a respectable list. Those are my motives.

"But I had no such motives at the beginning. Actually, there are never motives behind actions. All actions are fixed. What we called motives evidently are rationalizations by the helpless observing consciousness, which is intelligent enough to smell an event coming – and, since it cannot avert the event, instead cooks up reasons for wanting it to happen."

"Wow," Dr. Wald said, inelegantly but with considerable force.

"Either 'wow' or 'balderdash' seems to be called for – I can't quite decide which," Weinbaum agreed. "We know that Dana is an actress, Thor, so let's not fall off the apple tree quite yet. Dana, I've been saving the *really* hard question for the last. That question is: *How?* How did you arrive at this modification of the Dirac transmitter? Remember, we know your background, where we didn't know that of 'J. Shelby Stevens.' You're not a scientist. There were some fairly highpowered intellects among your distant relatives, but that's as close as you come."

"I'm going to give you several answers to that question," Dana Lje said. "Pick the one you like best. They're all true, but they tend to contradict each other here and there.

"To begin with, you're right about my relatives, of course. If you'll check your dossier again, though, you'll discover that those so-called 'distant' relatives were the last surviving members of my family besides myself. When they died, second and fourth and ninth cousins though they were, their estates reverted to me, and among their effects I found a sketch of a possible instantaneous communicator based on de Broglie-wave inversion. The material was in very rough form, and mostly beyond my comprehension, because I am, as you say, no scientist myself. But I was interested; I could see, dimly, what such a thing might be worth – and not only in money.

"My interest was fanned by two coincidences – the kind of coincidences that cause-and-effect just can't allow, but which seem to happen all the same in the world of unchangeable events. For most of my adult life, I've been in communications industries of one kind or another, mostly branches of video. I had communications equipment around me constantly, and I had coffee and doughnuts with communications engineers every day. First I picked up the jargon; then, some of the procedures; and eventually a little real knowledge. Some of the things I learned can't be gotten any other way. Some other things are ordinarily available only to highly educated people like Dr. Wald here, and came to me by accident, in horseplay, between kisses, and a hundred other ways – all natural to the environment of a video network."

Weinbaum found, to his own astonishment, that the "between kisses" clause did not sit very well in his chest. He said, with unintentional brusqueness: "What's the other coincidence?"

"A leak in your own staff."

"Dana, you ought to have that set to music."

"Suit yourself."

"I can't suit myself," Weinbaum said petulantly. "I work for the government. Was this leak direct to you?"

"Not at first. That was why I kept insisting to you in person that there might be such a leak, and why I finally began to hint about it in public, on my program. I was hoping that you'd be able to seal it up inside the bureau before my first rather tenuous contact with it got lost. When I didn't succeed in provoking you into protecting yourself, I took the risk of making direct contact with the leak myself – and the first piece of secret information that came to me through it was the final point I needed to put my Dirac communicator together. When it was all assembled, it did more than just communicate. It predicted. And I can tell you why."

Weinbaum said thoughtfully, "I don't find this very hard to accept, so far. Pruned of the philosophy, it even makes some sense of the 'J. Shelby Stevens' affair. I assume that by letting the old gentleman become known as somebody who knew more about the Dirac transmitter than I did, and who wasn't averse to negotiating with anybody who had money, you kept the leak working through you – rather than transmitting data directly to unfriendly governments."

"It did work out that way," Dana said. "But that wasn't

60

the genesis or the purpose of the Stevens masquerade. I've already given you the whole explanation of how that came about."

"Well, you'd better name me that leak, before the man gets away."

"When the price is paid, not before. It's too late to prevent a getaway, anyhow. In the meantime, Robin, I want to go on and tell you the other answer to your question about how I was able to find this particular Dirac secret, and you didn't. What answers I've given you up to now have been cause-and-effect answers, with which we're all more comfortable. But I want to impress on you that all apparent cause-and-effect relationships are accidents. There is no such thing as a cause, and no such thing as an effect. I found the secret because I found it; that event was fixed; that certain circumstances seem to explain why I found it, in the old cause-and-effect terms, is irrelevant. Similarly, with all your superior equipment and brains, you didn't find it for one reason, and one reason alone: because you didn't find it. The history of the future says you didn't."

"I pays my money and I takes no choice, eh?" Weinbaum said ruefully.

"I'm afraid so – and I don't like it any better than you do."

"Thor, what's your opinion of all this?"

"It's just faintly flabbergasting," Wald said soberly. "However, it hangs together. The deterministic universe which Miss Lje paints was a common feature of the old relativity theories, and as sheer speculation has an even longer history. I would say that, in the long run, how much credence we place in the story as a whole will rest upon her method of, as she calls it, reading the future. If it is demonstrable beyond any doubt, then the rest becomes perfectly credible – philosophy and all. If it doesn't, then what remains is an admirable job of acting, plus some metaphysics which, while self-consistent, is not original with Miss Lje."

"That sums up the case as well as if I'd coached you, Dr. Wald," Dana said. "I'd like to point out one more thing. If I can read the future, then 'J. Shelby Stevens' never had any need for a staff of field operatives, and he never needed to send a single Dirac message which you might intercept. All he needed to do was to make predictions from his readings, which he knew to be infallible; no private espionage network had to be involved."

"I see that," Weinbaum said dryly. "All right, Dana, let's put the proposition this way: *I do not believe you*. Much of what you say is probably true, but in totality I believe it to be false. On the other hand, if you're telling the whole truth, you certainly deserve a place on the bureau staff – it would be dangerous as hell *not* to have you with us – and the marriage is a more or less minor matter, except to you and me. You can have that with no strings attached; I don't want to be bought, any more than you would.

"So: if you will tell me where the leak is, we will consider that part of the question closed. I make that condition not as a price, but because I don't want to get myself engaged to somebody who might be shot as a spy within a month."

"Fair enough," Dana said. "Robin, your leak is Margaret Soames. She is an Erskine operative, and nobody's bubblebrain. She's a highly trained technician."

"Well, I'll be damned," Weinbaum said in astonishment. "Then she's already flown the coop – she was the one who first told me we'd identified you. She must have taken on that job in order to hold up delivery long enough to stage an exit."

"That's right. But you'll catch her, day after tomorrow. And you are now a hooked fish, Robin."

There was another suppressed burble from Thor Wald.

"I accept the fate happily," Weinbaum said, eying the gunsight knee. "Now, if you will tell me how you work your swami trick, and if it backs up everything you've said to the letter, as you claim, I'll see to it that you're also taken into the bureau and that all charges against you are quashed.

Otherwise, I'll probably have to kiss the bride between the bars of a cell."

Dana smiled. "The secret is very simple. It's in the beep."

Weinbaum's jaw dropped. "The beep? The Dirac noise?"

"That's right. You didn't find it out because you considered the beep to be just a nuisance, and ordered Miss Soames to cut it off all tapes before sending them in to you. Miss Soames, who had some inkling of what the beep meant, was more than happy to do so, leaving the reading of the beep exclusively to 'J. Shelby Stevens' – who she thought was going to take on Erskine as a client."

"Explain," Thor Wald said, looking intense.

"Just as you assumed, every Dirac message that is sent is picked up by every receiver that is capable of detecting it. *Every* receiver – including the first one ever built, which is yours, Dr. Wald, through the hundreds of thousands of them which will exist throughout the Galaxy in the twenty-fourth century, to the untold millions which will exist in the thirtieth century, and so on. The Dirac beep is the simultaneous reception of *every one of the Dirac messages which have ever been sent, or ever will be sent.* Incidentally, the cardinal number of the total of those messages is a relatively small and of course finite number; it's far below really large finite numbers such as the number of electrons in the universe, even when you break each and every message down into individual 'bits' and count those."

"Of course," Dr. Wald said softly. "Of course! But, Miss Lje . . . how do you tune for an individual message? We tried fractional positron frequencies, and got nowhere."

"I didn't even know fractional positron frequencies existed," Dana confessed. "No, it's simple – so simple that a lucky layman like me could arrive at it. You tune individual messages out of the beep by time lag, nothing more. All the messages arrive at the same instant, in the smallest fraction of time that exists, something called a 'chronon.'"

"Yes," Wald said. "The time it takes one electron to move from one quantum-level to another. That's the Pythagorean point of time measurement."

"Thank you. Obviously no gross physical receiver can respond to a message that brief, or at least that's what I thought at first. But because there are relay and switching delays, various forms of feedback and so on, in the apparatus itself, the beep arrives at the output end as a complex pulse which has been 'splattered' along the time axis for a full second or more. That's an effect which you can exaggerate by recording the 'splattered' beep on a high-speed tape, the same way you would record any event that you wanted to study in slow motion. Then you tune up the various failure-points in your receiver, to exaggerate one failure, minimize all the others, and use noise-suppressing techniques to cut out the background."

Thor Wald frowned. "You'd still have a considerable garble when you were through. You'd have to sample the messages —"

"Which is just what I did; Robin's little lecture to me about the ultrawave gave me that hint. I set myself to find out how the ultrawave channel carries so many messages at once, and I discovered that you people sample the incoming pulses every thousandth of a second and pass on one pip only when the wave deviates in a certain way from the mean. I didn't really believe it would work on the Dirac beep, but it turned out just as well: 90 percent as intelligible as the original transmission after it came through the smearing device. I'd already got enough from the beep to put my plan in motion, of course – but now every voice message in it was available, and crystal-clear: if you select three pips every thousandth of a second, you can even pick up an intelligible transmission of music – a little razzy, but good enough to identify the instruments that are playing – and that's a very close test of any communications device."

"There's a question of detail here that doesn't quite follow," said Weinbaum, for whom the technical talk was becoming a little too thick to fight through. "Dana, you say that you knew the course this conversation was going to take – yet it isn't being Dirac-recorded, nor can I see any reason why any summary of it would be sent out on the Dirac afterwards."

"That's true, Robin. However, when I leave here, I will make such a transcast myself, on my own Dirac. Obviously I will – because I've *already* picked it up, from the beep."

"In other words, you're going to call yourself up – months ago."

"That's it," Dana said. "It's not as useful a technique as you might think at first, because it's dangerous to make such broadcasts while a situation is still developing. You can safely 'phone back' details only after the given situation has gone to completion, as a chemist might put it. Once you know, however, that when you use the Dirac you're dealing with time, you can coax some very strange things out of the instrument."

She paused and smiled. "I have heard," she said conversationally, "the voice of the President of our Galaxy, in 3480, announcing the federation of the Milky Way and the Magellanic Clouds. I've heard the commander of a world-line cruiser, travelling from 8873 to 8704 along the world line of the planet Hathshepa, which circles a star on the rim of NGC 4725, calling for help across eleven million light-years – but what kind of help he was calling for, or will be calling for, is beyond my comprehension. And many other things. When you check on me, you'll hear these things too – and you'll wonder what many of them mean.

"And you'll listen to them even more closely than I did, in the hope of finding out whether or not anyone was able to understand in time to help."

Weinbaum and Wald looked dazed.

Her voice became a little more somber. "Most of the voices in the Dirac beep are like that – they're cries for help, which you can overhear decades or centuries before the senders get into trouble. You'll feel obligated to answer every one, to try to supply the help that's needed. And you'll listen to the succeeding messages and say: 'Did we – will we get there in time? Did we understand in time?'

"And in most cases you won't be sure. You'll know the future, but not what most of it means. The farther into the future you travel with the machine, the more incomprehensible the messages become, and so you're reduced to telling yourself that time will, after all, have to pass by at its own pace, before enough of the surrounding events can emerge to make those remote messages clear.

"The long-run effect, as far as I can think it through, is not going to be that of omniscience – of our consciousness being extracted entirely from the time stream and allowed to view its whole sweep from one side. Instead, the Dirac in effect simply slides the bead of consciousness forward from the present a certain distance. Whether it's five hundred or five thousand years still remains to be seen. At that point the law of diminishing returns sets in – or the noise factor begins to overbalance the information, take your choice – and the observer is reduced to travelling in time at the same old speed. He's just a bit ahead of himself."

"You've thought a great deal about this," Wald said slowly. "I dislike to think of what might have happened had some less conscientious person stumbled on the beep."

"That wasn't in the cards," Dana said.

In the ensuing quiet, Weinbaum felt a faint, irrational sense of let-down, of something which had promised more than had been delivered – rather like the taste of fresh bread as compared to its smell, or the discovery that Thor Wald's Swedish 'folk song' Nat-og-Dag was only Cole Porter's *Night and Day* in another language. He recognized the feeling: it was the usual emotion of the hunter when the hunt is over, the born detective's professional version of the *post coitum tristre*. After looking at the smiling, supple Dana Lje a moment more, however, he was almost content.

"There is one more thing," he said. "I don't want to be

66

insufferably skeptical about this – but I want to see it work. Thor, can we set up a sampling and smearing device such as Dana describes and run a test?"

"In fifteen minutes," Dr. Wald said. "We have most of the unit in already assembled form on our big ultrawave receiver, and it shouldn't take any effort to add a high-speed tape unit to it. I'll do it right now."

He went out. Weinbaum and Dana looked at each other for a moment, rather like strange cats. Then the security officer got up, with what he knew to be an air of somewhat grim determination, and seized his fiancée's hands, anticipating a struggle.

That first kiss was, by intention at least, mostly *pro forma*. But by the time Wald padded back into the office, the letter had been pretty thoroughly superseded by the spirit. The scientist harrumphed and set his burden on the desk. "This is all there is to it," he said, "but I had to hunt all through the library to find a Dirac record with a beep still on it. Just a moment more while I make connections . . ."

Weinbaum used the time to bring his mind back to the matter at hand, although not quite completely. Then two tape spindles began to whir like so many bees, and the end-stopped sound of the Dirac beep filled the room. Wald stopped the apparatus, reset it, and started the smearing tape very slowly in the opposite direction.

A distant babble of voices came from the speaker. As Weinbaum leaned forward tensely, one voice said clearly and loudly above the rest:

"Hello, Earth bureau. Lt. T. L. Matthews at Hercules Station NGC 6341, transmission date 13–22–2091. We have the last point on the orbit curve of your dope-runners plotted, and the curve itself points to a small system about twenty-five light-years from the base here; the place hasn't even got a name on our charts. Scouts show the home planet at least twice as heavily fortified as we anticipated, so we'll need another cruiser. We have a 'can-do' from you in the beep for us, but we're waiting as ordered to get it in the present. NGC 6341 Matthews out."

After the first instant of stunned amazement – for no amount of intellectual willingness to accept could have prepared him for the overwhelming fact itself – Weinbaum had grabbed a pencil and begun to write at top speed. As the voice signed out he threw the pencil down and looked excitedly at Dr. Wald.

"Seven months ahead," he said, aware that he was grinning like an idiot. "Thor, you know the trouble we've had with that needle in the Hercules haystack! This orbit-curve trick must be something Matthews has yet to dream up – at least he hasn't come to me with it yet, and there's nothing in the situation as it stands now that would indicate a closing time of six months for the case. The computers said it would take three more years."

"It's new data," Dr. Wald agreed solemnly.

"Well, don't stop there, in God's name! Let's hear some more!"

Dr. Wald went through the ritual, much faster this time. The speaker said:

"Nausentampen. Eddettompic. Berobsilom. Aimkak-setchoc. Sanbetogmow. Datdectamset. Domatrosmin Out."

"My word," Wald said. "What's all that?"

"That's what I was talking about," Dana Lje said. "At least half of what you get from the beep is just as incomprehensible. I suppose it's whatever has happened to the English language, thousands of years from now."

"No, it isn't," Weinbaum said. He had resumed writing, and was still at it, despite the comparative briefness of the transmission. "Not this sample, anyhow. That, ladies and gentlemen, is code – no language consists exclusively of four-syllable words, of that you can be sure. What's more, it's a version of our code. I can't break it down very far – it takes a full-time expert to read this stuff – but I get the date and some of the sense. It's March 12, 3022, and there's some kind of a

68

mass evacuation taking place. The message seems to be a routing order."

"But why will we be using code?" Dr. Wald wanted to know. "It implies that we think somebody might overhear us – somebody else with a Dirac. That could be very messy."

"It could indeed," Weinbaum said. "But we'll find out, I imagine. Give her another spin, Thor."

"Shall I try for a picture this time?"

Weinbaum nodded. A moment later, he was looking squarely into the green-skinned face of something that looked like an animated traffic signal with a helmet on it. Though the creature had no mouth, the Dirac speaker was saying quite clearly, "Hello, Chief. This is Thammos NGC 2287, transmission date Gor 60, 302 by my calendar, July 2, 2973 by yours. This is a lousy little planet. Everything stinks of oxygen, just like Earth. But the natives accept us and that's the important thing. We've got your genius safely born. Detailed report coming later by paw. NGC 2287 Thammos out."

"I wish I knew my New General Catalogue better," Weinbaum said. "Isn't that M 41 in Canis Major, the one with the red star in the middle? And we'll be using non-humanoids there! What *was* that creature, anyhow? Never mind, spin her again."

Dr. Wald spun her again. Weinbaum, already feeling a little dizzy, had given up taking notes. That could come later, all that could come later. Now he wanted only scenes and voices, more and more scenes and voices from the future. They were better than aquavit, even with a beer chaser.

IV

The indoctrination tape ended, and Krasna touched a button. The Dirac screen darkened, and folded silently back into the desk.

"They didn't see their way through to us, not by a long shot," he said. "They didn't see, for instance, that when one section of the government becomes nearly all-knowing – no matter how small it was to begin with – it necessarily becomes all of the government that there is. Thus the bureau turned into the Service and pushed everyone else out.

"On the other hand, those people did come to be afraid that a government with an all-knowing arm might become a rigid dictatorship. That couldn't happen and didn't happen, because the more you know, the wider your field of possible operation becomes and the more fluid and dynamic a society you need. How could a rigid society expand to other star systems, let alone other galaxies? It couldn't be done."

"I should think it could," Jo said slowly. "After all, if you know in advance what everybody is going to do . . ."

"But we don't, Jo. That's just a popular fiction – or, if you like, a red herring. Not all of the business of the cosmos is carried on over the Dirac, after all. The only events we can ever overhear are those which are transmitted as a message. Do you order your lunch over the Dirac? Of course you don't. Up to now, you've never said a word over the Dirac in your life.

"And there's much more to it than that. All dictatorships are based on the proposition that government can somehow control a man's thoughts. We know now that the consciousness of the observer is the only free thing in the Universe. Wouldn't we look foolish trying to control that, when our entire physics shows that it's impossible to do so? That's why the Service is in no sense a thought police. We're interested only in acts. We're an Event Police."

"But why?" Jo said. "If all history is fixed, why do we bother with these boy-meets-girl assignments, for instance? The meetings will happen anyhow."

"Of course they will," Krasna agreed immediately. "But look, Jo. Our interests as a government depend upon the future. We operate *as if* the future is as real as the past, and so far we haven't been disappointed: the Service is 100 per cent

70

successful. But that very success isn't without its warnings. What would happen if we *stopped* supervising events? We don't know, and we don't dare take the chance. Despite the evidence that the future is fixed, we have to take on the role of the caretaker of inevitability. We believe that nothing can possibly go wrong . . . but we have to act on the philosophy that history helps only those who help themselves.

"That's why we safeguard huge numbers of courtships right through to contract, and even beyond it. We have to see to it that *every single person who is mentioned in any Dirac 'cast gets born*. Our obligation as Event Police is to make the events of the future possible, because those events are crucial to our society – even the smallest of them. It's an enormous task, believe me, and it gets bigger and bigger every day. Apparently it always will."

"Always?" Jo said. "What about the public? Isn't it going to smell this out sooner or later? The evidence is piling up at a terrific rate."

"Yes and no," Krasna said. "Lots of people are smelling it out right now, just as you did. But the number of new people we need in the Service grows faster – it's always ahead of the number of laymen who follow the clues to the truth."

Jo took a deep breath. "You take all this as if it were as commonplace as boiling an egg, Kras," he said. "Don't you ever wonder about some of the things you get from the beep? That 'cast Dana Lje picked up from Canes Venatici, for instance, the one from the ship that was travelling backward in time? How is that possible? What could be the purpose? Is it —"

"*Pace, pace*," Krasna said. "I don't know and I don't care. Neither should you. That event is too far in the future for us to worry about. We can't possibly know its context yet, so there's no sense in trying to understand it. If an Englishman of around 1600 had found out about the American Revolution, he would have thought it a tragedy; an Englishman of 1950 would have a very different view of

71

it. We're in the same spot. The messages we get from the really far future have no contexts as yet."

"I think I see," Jo said. "I'll get used to it in time, I suppose, after I use the Dirac for a while. Or does my new rank authorise me to do that?"

"Yes, it does. But, Jo, first I want to pass on to you a rule of Service etiquette that must never be broken. You won't be allowed anywhere near a Dirac mike until you have it burned into your memory beyond any forgetfulness."

"I'm listening, Kras, believe me."

"Good. This is the rule: *The date of a Serviceman's death must never be mentioned in a Dirac 'cast.*"

Jo blinked, feeling a little chilly. The reason behind the rule was decidedly tough-minded, but its ultimate kindness was plain. He said, "I won't forget that. I'll want that protection myself. Many thanks, Kras. What's my new assignment?"

"To begin with," Krasna said, grinning, "as simple a job as I've ever given you, right here on Randolph. Skin out of here and find me that cab driver – the one who mentioned time-travel to you. He's uncomfortably close to the truth; closer than you were in one category.

"Find him, and bring him to me. The Service is about to take in a new raw recruit!"

The Box

When Meister got out of bed that Tuesday morning, he thought it was before dawn. He rarely needed an alarm clock these days – a little light in his eyes was enough to awaken him and sometimes his dreams brought him upright long before the sun came up.

It had seemed a reasonably dreamless night, but probably he had just forgotten the dreams. Anyhow, here he was, awake early. He padded over to the window, shut it, pulled up the blind and looked out.

The street lights were not off yet, but the sky was already a smooth, dark gray. Meister had never before seen such a sky. Even the dullest overcast before a snowfall shows some variation in brightness. The sky here – what he could see of it between the apartment houses – was like the inside of a lead helmet.

He shrugged and turned away, picking up the clock from the table to turn off the alarm. Some day, he promised himself, he would sleep long enough to hear it ring. That would be a good day; it would mean that the dreams were gone. In Concentration Camp Dora, one had awakened the moment the tunnel lights were put on; otherwise one might be beaten awake, or dead. Meister was deaf in the left ear on that account. For the first three days at Dora he had had to be awakened.

He became aware suddenly that he was staring fixedly at the face of the clock, his subconscious ringing alarm bells of its own. *Nine o'clock!* No, it was not possible. It was

73

obviously close to sunrise. He shook the clock stupidly, although it was ticking and had been since he first noticed it. Tentatively he touched the keys at the back.

The alarm had run down.

This was obviously ridiculous. The clock was wrong. He put it back on the table and turned on the little radio. After a moment it responded with a terrific thrumming, as if a vacuum cleaner were imprisoned in its workings.

"B-flat," Meister thought automatically. He had only one good ear, but he still had perfect pitch – a necessity for a resonance engineer. He shifted the setting. The hum got louder. Hastily he reversed the dial. Around 830 kc, where WNYC came in, the hum was almost gone, but of course it was too early yet for the city station to be on the air —

". . . in your homes," a voice struck in clearly above the humming. "We are awaiting a report from Army headquarters. In the meantime, any crowding at the boundaries of the barrier will interrupt the work of the Mayor's inquiry commission . . . Here's a word just in from the Port Authority: all ferry service has been suspended until further notice. Subways and tubes are running outbound trains only; however, local service remains normal so far."

Barrier? Meister went to the window again and looked out. The radio voice continued:

"NBC at Radio City disclaims all knowledge of the persistent signal which has blotted out radio programs from nine hundred kilocycles on up since midnight last night. This completes the roster of broadcasting stations in the city proper. It is believed that the tone is associated with the current wall around Manhattan and most of the other boroughs. Some outside stations are still getting through, but at less than a fiftieth of their normal input." The voice went on:

"At Columbia University, the dean of the Physics Department estimates that about the same proportion of sunlight is also getting through. We do not yet have any report about the passage of air through the barrier. The flow of water in the portions of the East and Hudson Rivers which lie under the screen is said to be normal, and no abnormalities are evident at the Whitehall Street tidal station."

There was a pause; the humming went on unabated. Then there was a sharp *beep!* and the voice said, "At the signal – 9 A.M., Eastern Daylight Savings Time."

Meister left the radio on while he dressed. The alarming pronouncements kept on, but he was not yet thoroughly disturbed, except for Ellen. She might be frightened; but probably nothing more serious would happen. Right now, he should be at the labs. If the Team had put this thing up overnight, they would tease him unmercifully for sleeping through the great event.

The radio continued to reel off special notices, warnings, new bulletins. The announcer sounded as if he were on the thin edge of hysteria; evidently he had not yet been told what it was all about. Meister was tying his left shoe when he realized that the reports were beginning to sound much worse.

"From LaGuardia Field we have just been notified that an experimental plane has been flown through the barrier at a point over the jammed Triboro Bridge. It has not appeared over the city and is presumed lost. On the *Miss New York* disaster early this morning we still have no complete report. Authorities on Staten Island say the ferry ordinarily carried less than two hundred passengers at that hour, but thus far only eleven have been picked up. One of these survivors was brought in to a Manhattan slip by the tub *Marjorie Q*; he is still in a state of extreme shock and Bellevue Hospital says no statement can be expected from him until tomorrow. It appears, however, that he swam *under* the barrier."

His voice carried the tension he evidently felt. "Outside the screen a heavy fog still prevails – the same fog which hid the barrier from the ferry captain until his ship was destroyed almost to the midpoint. The Police

75

Department has again requested that all New Yorkers stay — "

Alarmed at last, Meister switched off the machine and left the apartment, locking it carefully. Unless those idiots turned off their screen, there would be panic and looting before the day was out.

Downstairs in the little grocery there was a mob arguing in low, terrified voices, their faces as gray as the ominous sky. He pushed through them to the phone.

The grocer was sitting behind it. "Phone service is tied up, Mr. Meister," he said hoarsely.

"I can get through, I think. What has happened?"

"Some foreign enemy, is *my* guess. There's a big dome of somethin' all around the city. Nobody can get in or out. You stick your hand in, you draw back a bloody stump. Stuff put through on the other side don't come through." He picked up the phone with a trembling hand and passed it over. "Good luck."

Meister dialed Ellen first. He needed to know if she were badly frightened, and to reassure her if she were. Nothing happened for a while; then an operator said, "I'm sorry, sir, but there will be no private calls for the duration of the emergency, unless you have a priority."

"Give me Emergency Code B-Nineteen, then," Meister said.

"Your group, sir?"

"Screen Team."

There was a faint sound at the outer end of the line, as if the girl had taken a quick breath. "Yes, sir," she said. "Right away." There was an angry crackle, and then the droning when the number was being rung.

"Screen Team," a voice said.

"Resonance section, please," Meister said, and when he was connected and had identified himself, a voice growled:

"Hello, Jake, this is Frank Schafer. Where the deuce are you? I sent you a telegram – but I suppose you didn't get it, the boards are jammed. Get on down here, quick!"

"No, I haven't any telegram," Meister said. "Whom do I congratulate?"

"Nobody, you fool! *We* didn't do this. We don't even know how it's been done!"

Meister felt the hairs on the back of his neck stirring. It was as if he were back in the tunnels of Concentration Camp Dora again. He swallowed and said, "But it is the antibomb screen?"

"The very thing," Schafer's tinny voice said bitterly. "Only somebody else has beat us to it – and we're trapped under it."

"It's really bombproof – you're sure of that?"

"It's anything-proof! Nothing can pass it! *And we can't get out of it, either!*"

It took quite a while to get the story straight. Project B-19, the meaningless label borne by the top-secret, billion-dollar Atomic Defense Project, was in turmoil. Much of its laboratory staff had been in the field or in Washington when the thing happened, and the jam in phone service had made it difficult to get the men who were still in the city back to the central offices.

"It's like this," Frank Schafer said, kneading a chunk of art gum rapidly. "This dome went up last night. It lets in a little light and a few of the strongest outside radio stations near by. But that's all – or anyhow, all that we've been able to establish so far. It's a perfect dome, over the whole island and parts of the other boroughs and New Jersey. It doesn't penetrate the ground or the water, but the only really big water frontage is way out in the harbor, so that lets out much chance of everybody swimming under it like that man from the *Miss New York*."

"The subways are running, I heard," Meister said.

"Sure; we can evacuate the city if we have to, but not fast enough." The mobile fingers crumbled bits off the sides of the art gum. "It won't take long to breathe up the air here, and if any fires start it'll be worse. Also there's a layer of ozone about twenty feet deep all along the inside of the barrier – but don't ask me why! Even if we don't have any big blazes, we're losing oxygen at a terrific rate by ozone-fixing and surface oxidation of the ionized area."

"Ionized?" Meister frowned. "Is there much?"

"Plenty!" Schafer said. "We haven't let it out, but in another twenty hours you won't be able to hear anything on the radio but a noise like a tractor climbing a pile of cornflakes. There's been an increase already. Whatever we're using for ether these days is building up tension fast."

A runner came in from the private wires and dropped a flimsy on Frank's desk. The physicist looked at it quickly, then passed it to Meister.

"That's what I figured. You can see the spot we're in."

The message reported that oxygen was diffusing inward through the barrier at about the same rate as might be accounted for by osmosis. The figures on loss of CO_2 were less easy to establish, but it appeared that the rate here was also of an osmotic order of magnitude. It was signed by a top-notch university chemist.

"Impossible!" Meister said.

"No, it's so. And New York is entirely too big a cell to live, Jake. If we're getting oxygen only osmotically, we'll be suffocated in a week. And did you ever hear of semipermeable membrane passing a lump of coal, or a tomato? Air, heat, food – all cut off."

"What does the Army say?"

"What they usually say: 'Do something, on the double!' We're lucky we're civilians, or we'd be court-martialed for dying!" Schafer laughed angrily and pitched the art gum away. "It's a very pretty problem, in a way," he said. "We have our antibomb screen. Now we have to find how to make ourselves *vulnerable* to the bomb – or cash in our chips. And in six days — "

The phone jangled and Schafer snatched at it. "Yeah, this

is Dr. Schafer . . . I'm sorry, Colonel, but we have every available man called in now except those on the Mayor's commission . . . No, I don't know. Nobody knows, yet. We're tracing that radio signal now. If it has anything to do with the barrier, we'll be able to locate the generator and destroy it."

The physicist slammed the phone into its cradle and glared at Meister. "I've been taking this phone stuff all morning! I wish you'd showed up earlier. Here's the picture, briefly: The city is dying. Telephone and telegraph lines give us some communication with the outside, and we will be able to use radio inside the dome for a little while longer. There are teams outside trying to crack the barrier, but all the significant phenomena are taking place inside. Out there it just looks like a big black dome – no radiation effects, no ionization, no radio tone, no nothin'!

"We are evacuating now," he went on, "but if the dome stays up, over three quarters of the trapped people will die. If there's any fire or violence, almost all of us will die."

"You talk," Meister said, "as if you want me to kill the screen all by myself."

Schafer grinned nastily. "Sure, Jake! This barrier obviously doesn't act specifically on nuclear reactions; it stops almost everything. Almost everyone here is a nuclear man, as useless for this problem as a set of cooky-cutters. Every fact we've gotten so far shows this thing to be an immense and infinitely complicated form of cavity-resonance – and you're the only resonance engineer inside."

The grin disappeared. Schafer said, "We can give you all the electronics technicians you need, plenty of official backing, and general theoretical help. It's not much but it's all we've got. We estimate about eleven million people inside this box – eleven million corpses unless you can get the lid off it."

Meister nodded. Somehow, the problem did not weigh as heavily upon him as it might have. He was remembering Dora, the wasted bodies jammed under the stairs, in

79

storerooms, fed into the bake-oven five at a time. One could survive almost anything if one had had practice in surviving. There was only Ellen —

Ellen was probably in The Box – the dome. That meant something, while eleven million was only a number.

"*Entdecken,*" he murmured.

Schafer looked up at him, his blue eyes snapping sparks. Schafer certainly didn't look like one of the world's best nuclear physicists. Schafer was a sandy-haired runt – with the bomb hung over his head by a horsehair.

"What's that?" he said.

"A German word," Meister answered. "It means, to discover – literally, to take the roof off. That is the first step, it seems. To take the roof off, we must discover that transmitter."

"I've got men out with loop antennae. The geometrical center of the dome is right at the tip of the Empire State Building, but WNBT says there's nothing up there but their television transmitters."

"What they mean," Meister said, "is that there was nothing else up there two weeks ago. There *must* be a radiator at a radiant point no matter how well it is disguised."

"I'll send a team." Schafer got up, fumbling for the art gum he had thrown away. "I'll go myself, I guess. I'm jittery here."

"With your teeth? I would not advise it. You would die slain, as the Italians say!"

"Teeth?" Schafer said. He giggled nervously. "What's that got to — "

"You have metal in your mouth. If the mast is actually radiating this effect, your jawbones might be burnt out of your head. Get a group with perfect teeth, or porcelain fillings at best. And wear nothing with metal in it, not even shoes."

"Oh," Schafer said. "I knew we needed you, Jake." He rubbed the back of his hand over his forehead and reached into his shirt pocket for a cigarette.

Meister struck it out of his hand. "Six days' oxygen remaining," he said.

Schafer lunged up out of his chair, aimed a punch at Meister's head, and fainted across the desk.

The dim city stank of ozone. The street lights were still on. Despite radioed warnings to stay indoors surging mobs struggled senselessly toward the barrier. Counterwaves surged back, coughing, from the unbreathable stuff pouring out from it. More piled up in subway stations; people screamed and trampled one another. Curiously, the city's take that day was enormous. Not even disaster could break the deeply entrenched habit of putting a token in the turnstile.

The New York Central and Long Island Railroads, whose tracks were above ground where the screen cut across them, were shut down, as were the underground lines which came to the surface inside The Box. Special trains were running every three minutes from Pennsylvania Station, with passengers jamming the aisles and platforms.

In the Hudson Tubes the situation was worse. So great was the crush of fleeing humans there, they could hardly operate at all. The screen drew a lethal line between Hoboken and Newark, so that Tube trains had to make the longer of the two trips to get their passengers out of The Box. A brief power interruption stopped one train in complete darkness for ten minutes beneath the Hudson River, and terror and madness swept through it.

Queens and Brooklyn subways siphoned off a little pressure, but only a little. In a major disaster the normal human impulse is to go north, on the map-fostered myth that north is "up."

Navy launches were readied to ferry as many as cared to make the try out to where The Box lay over the harbor and the rivers, but thus far there were no such swimmers. Very few people can swim twenty feet under water, and to come up for air short of that twenty feet would be disastrous.

That would be as fatal as coming up in the barrier itself; ozone is lung-rot in high concentrations. That alone kept most of the foolhardy from trying to run through the wall – that, and the gasmasked police cordon.

From Governor's Island, about half of which was in The Box, little Army ferries shipped over several cases of small arms which were distributed to subway and railroad guards. Two detachments of infantry also came along, relieving a little of the strain on the police.

Meister, hovering with two technicians and the helicopter pilot over a building on the edge of the screen, peered downward in puzzlement. It was hard to make any sense of the geometry of shadows below him.

"Give me the phone," he said.

The senior technician passed him the mike. A comparatively long-wave channel had been cleared by a major station for the use of emergency teams and prowl cars, since nothing could be heard on short-wave above that eternal humming.

"Frank, are you on?" Meister called. "Any word from Ellen yet?"

"No, but her landlady says she went to Jersey to visit yesterday," came over the airwaves. There was an unspoken understanding between them that the hysterical attack of an hour ago would not be mentioned. "You'll have to crack The Box to get more news, I guess, Jake. See anything yet?"

"Nothing but more trouble. Have you thought yet about heat conservation? I am reminded that it is summer; we will soon have an oven here."

"I thought of that, but it isn't so," Frank Schafer's voice said. "It seems hotter only because there's no wind. Actually, the Weather Bureau says we're *losing* heat pretty rapidly; they expect the drop to level at fifteen to twenty above."

Meister whistled. "So low! Yet there is a steady supply of calories in the water — "

"Water's a poor conductor. What worries me is this accursed ozone. It's diffusing through the city – already smells like the inside of a transformer around here!"

"What about the Empire State Building?"

"Not a thing. We ran soap bubbles along the power leads to see if something was tapping some of WNBT's power, but there isn't a break in them anywhere. Maybe you'd better go over there when you're through at the barrier. There are some things we can't make sense of."

"I shall," Meister said. "I will leave here as soon as I start a fire."

Schafer began to sputter. Meister smiled gently and handed the phone back to the technician.

"Break out the masks," he said. "We can go down now."

A rooftop beside the barrier was like some hell dreamed up in the violent ward of a hospital. Every movement accumulated a small static charge on the surface of the body, which discharged stingingly and repeatedly from the fingertips and even the tip of the nose if it approached a grounded object too closely.

Only a few yards away was the unguessable wall itself, smooth, deep gray, featureless, yet somehow quivering with a pseudo-life of its own – a shimmering haze just too dense to penetrate. It had no definite boundary. Instead, the tarpaper over which it lay here began to dim, and within a foot faded into the general mystery.

Meister looked at the barrier. The absence of anything upon which the eye could fasten was dizzying. The mind made up patterns and flashes of lurid color and projected them into the grayness. Sometimes it seemed that the fog extended for miles. A masked policeman stepped over from the inside parapet and touched him on the elbow.

"Wouldn't look at her too long, sir," he said. "We've had ambulances below carting away sightseers who forgot to look away. Pretty soon your eyes sort of get fixed."

Meister nodded. The thing was hypnotic all right. And yet the eye was drawn to it because it was the only source of light here. The ionization was so intense that it bled off power from the lines, so that street lamps had gone off all around the edge. From the helicopter, the city had looked as if its rim was inked out in a vast ring. Meister could feel the individual hairs all over his body stirring; it made him feel infested. Well, there'd been no shortage of lice at Dora!

Behind him the technicians were unloading the apparatus from the 'copter. Meister beckoned. "Get a reading on field strength first of all," he said gloomily. "Whoever is doing this has plenty of power. Ionized gas, a difficult achievement — "

He stopped suddenly. Not so difficult. The city was enclosed; it was, in effect, a giant Geissler tube. Of course the concentration of rare gases was not high enough to produce a visible glow, but —

"Plenty high," the technician with the loop said. "Between forty-five and fifty thousand. Seems to be rising a little, too."

"Between — " Meister stepped quickly to the instrument. Sure enough, the black needle was wavering, so rapidly as to be only a fan-shaped blur between the two figures. "This is ridiculous! Is that instrument reliable?"

"I just took the underwriters' seal off it," the technician said. "Did you figure this much ozone could be fixed out without any alteration?"

"Yes, I had presupposed the equivalent of UV bombardment. This changes things. No wonder there is light leaking through that screen! Sergeant — "

"Yes sir?" the policeman mumbled through his mask.

"How much of the area below can you clear?"

"As much as you need."

"Good." Meister reached into his jacket pocket and produced the map of the city the pilot had given him. "We are here, yes? Make a cordon, then, from here to here." His soft pencil scrawled a black line around four buildings.

"Then get as much fire-fighting equipment outside the line as you can muster."

"You're expecting a bad fire?"

"No, a *good* one. But hurry!"

The cop scratched his head in puzzlement, but he went below. Meister smiled. Members of the Screen Team were the Mister Bigs in this city now. Twenty hours ago nobody'd ever heard of the Screen Team.

The technician, working with nervous quickness, was tying an oscilloscope into the loop circuit. Meister nodded approvingly. If there was a pulse to this phenomenon, it would be just as well to know its form. He snapped his fingers.

"What's wrong, doctor?"

"My memory. I have put my head on backwards when I got up this morning, I think. We will have to photograph the wave form; it will be too complex to analyse here."

"How do you know?" the technician asked.

"By that radio tone," Meister said. "You Americans work by sight. There are almost no resonance electronics men in this country. But in Germany we worked as much by ear as by eye. Where you convert a wave into a visible pattern, we turned it into an audible one. We had a saying that resonance engineers were disappointed musicians."

The face of the tube suddenly produced a green wiggle. It was the kind of wiggle a crazy man might make. The technician looked at it in dismay. "That," he said, "doesn't exist. I won't work in a science where it *could* exist!"

Meister grinned. "That is what I meant. The radio sound was a fundamental B-flat, but with hundreds of harmonics and overtones. You don't have it all in the field yet."

"I don't?" He looked. "So I don't! But when I reduce it that much, you can't see the shape of the modulations."

"We will have to photograph it by sections."

Bringing over the camera, the other man set it up. They worked rapidly, oppressed by the unnatural pearly glimmer, the masks, the stink of ozone which crept in at the sides of the treated cloth, the electrical prickling, above all by the silent terror of any trapped animal.

While they worked, the cop came back and stood by silently, watching. The gas mask gave no indication of his expression, but Meister could feel the pressure of faith radiating from the man. Doubtless these bits of equipment were meaningless to him – but bits of equipment like these had put up The Box, beyond the powers of policemen or presidents to take down again. Men who knew about such things were as good as gods now.

Unless they failed.

"That does it," the technician said.

The cop stepped forward. "I've got the area you marked roped off," he said diffidently. "We've searched the apartments and there's nobody in them. If there's any fire here, we'll be able to control it."

"Excellent!" Meister said. "Remember that this gas will feed the flames, however. You will need every possible man."

"Yes, sir. Anything else?"

"Just get out of the district yourself."

Meister climbed into the plane and stood by the open hatch, looking at his wrist watch. He gave the cop ten minutes to leave the tenement and get out to the fire lines. Then he struck a match and pitched it out onto the roof.

"Up!" he shouted.

The rotors roared. The pitch on the roof began to smolder. A tongue of flame shot up. In three seconds the whole side of the roof nearest the gray screen was blazing.

The helicopter lurched and clawed for altitude.

Behind the plane arose a brilliant and terrifying yellow glare. Meister didn't bother to watch it. He squatted with his back to the fire and waved pieces of paper over the neck of a bottle.

The ammonia fumes were invisible and couldn't be smelled through the mask, but on the dry-plates wiggly lines were appearing. Meister studied them, nibbling gently at his lower lip. With luck, the lines would answer one question at least: they would tell what The Box was. With luck, they might even tell how it was produced.

They would *not* tell where it came from.

The motion of the 'copter changed suddenly, and Meister's stomach stirred uneasily under his belt. He stowed the plates and looked up. The foreshortened spire of the Empire State Building pointed up at him through the transparent deck; another 'copter hovered at its tip. The television antennae were hidden now in what seemed to be a globe of some dark substance.

Meister picked up the radio-phone. "Schafer?" he called – this to the Empire State Building.

"No, this is Talliafero," came back an answer. "Schafer's back at the labs. We're about ready to leave. Need any help?"

"I don't think so," Meister said. "Is that foil you have around the tower mast?"

"Yes, but it's only a precaution. The whole tower's radiating. The foil radiates, too, now that we've got it up. See you later."

The other 'copter stirred and swooped away.

Meister twisted the dial up into the short-wave region. The humming surged in; he valved down the volume and listened intently. The sound was different somehow. After a moment his mind placed it. The fundamental B-flat was still there, but some of the overtones were gone; that meant that hundreds of them, which the little amplifier could not reproduce, were also gone. He was listening on an FM set; his little table set at the apartment was AM. So the wave was modulated along both axes, and probably pulse-modulated as well. But why would it simplify as one approached its source?

Resonance, of course. The upper harmonics were echoes. Yet a simple primary tone in a well-known frequency range couldn't produce The Box by itself. It was the harmonics that made the difference, and the harmonics couldn't appear without the existence of some chamber like The Box. Along this line of reasoning, The Box was a precondition of its own existence. Meister felt his head swimming.

"Hey," the pilot said. "It's started to snow!"

Meister turned off the set and looked out. "All right, let's go home now."

Despite its depleted staff, the Screen Team was quiet with the intense hush of concentration that was its equivalent of roaring activity. Frank Schafer's door was closed, but Meister didn't bother to knock. He was on the edge of an idea and there was no time to be lost in formalities.

There were a number of uniformed men in the office with Frank. There was also a big man in expensive clothes, and a smaller man who looked as if he needed sleep. The smaller man had dark circles under his eyes, but despite his haggardness Meister knew him. The mayor. The big man did not look familiar – nor pleasant.

As for the high brass, nothing in a uniform looked pleasant to Meister. He pushed forward and put the dry-plates down on Schafer's desk. "The resonance products," he said. "If we can duplicate the fundamental in the lab — "

There came a roar from the big man. "Dr. Schafer, is this the man we've been waiting for?"

Schafer made a tired gesture. "Jake, this is Roland Dean," he said. "You know the mayor, I think. These others are security officers. They seem to think you made The Box."

Meister stiffened. "I? That's idiotic!"

"Any noncitizen is automatically under suspicion," one of the Army men said. "However, Dr. Schafer exaggerates. We just want to ask a few questions."

The mayor coughed. He was obviously tired, and the taint of ozone did not make breathing very comfortable.

"I'm afraid there's more to it than that, Dr. Meister," he added. "Mr. Dean here has insisted upon an arrest. I'd like to say for myself that I think it all quite stupid."

88

"Thank you," Meister said. "What is Mr. Dean's interest in this?"

"Mr. Dean," Schafer growled, "is the owner of that block of tenements you're burning out up north. The fire's spreading, by the way. When I told him I didn't know why you lit it, he blew his top."

"Why not?" Dean said, glaring at Meister. "I fail to see why this emergency should be made an excuse for irresponsible destruction of property. Have you any reason for burning my buildings, Meister?"

"Are you having any trouble with breathing, Mr. Dean?" Meister asked.

"Certainly! Who isn't? Do you think you can make it easier for us by filling The Box with smoke?"

Meister nodded. "I gather that you have no knowledge of elementary chemistry, Mr. Dean. The Box is rapidly converting our oxygen into an unbreathable form. A good hot fire will consume some of it, but it will also break up the ozone molecules. The ratio is about two atoms of oxygen consumed for every one set free – out of three which in the form of ozone could not have been breathed at all."

Schafer sighed gustily. "I should have guessed. A neat scheme, Jake. But what about the ratio between reduction of ozone and over-all oxygen consumption?"

"Large enough to maintain five of the six days' grace with which we started. Had we let the ozone-fixing process continue unabated, we should not have lasted forty hours longer."

"Mumbo jumbo!" Dean said stonily, turning to Schafer. "A halfway measure. The problem is to get us out of this mess, not to stretch our sufferings out by three days by invading property rights. This man is a German, probably a Nazi! By your own admission, he's the only man in your whole section who's seemed to know what to do. And nothing he's done so far has shown any result, except to destroy some of my buildings!"

"Dr. Meister, just what *has* been accomplished thus far?" a colonel of Intelligence said.

"Only a few tentative observations," Meister said. "We have most of the secondary phenomena charted."

"Charts!" Dean snorted.

"Can you offer any assurance that The Box will be down in time?" the colonel asked.

"That," Meister said, "would be very foolish of me. The possibility exists, that is all. Certainly it will take time – we have barely scratched the surface."

"In that case, I'm afraid you'll have to consider yourself under arrest — "

"See here, Colonel!" Schafer surged to his feet, his face flushed. "Don't you know that he's the only man in The Box who can crack it? That fire was good common sense. If you arrest my men for *not* doing anything, we'll never get anything done!"

"I am not exactly stupid, Dr. Schafer," the colonel said harshly. "I have no interest in Mr. Dean's tenements, and if the mayor is forced to jail Dr. Meister we will spring him at once. All I'm interested in is the chance that Dr. Meister may be *maintaining* The Box instead of trying to *crack it*."

"Explain, please," Meister said mildly.

Pulling himself up to military straightness, the colonel cleared his throat and said:

"You're inside The Box. If you put it up, you have a way out of it, and know where the generator is. You may go where you please, but from now on we'll have a guard with you . . . Satisfied, Dr. Schafer?"

"It doesn't satisfy me!" Dean rumbled. "What about my property? Are you going to let this madman burn buildings with a guard to help?"

The colonel looked at the landlord. "Mr. Dean," he said quietly, "you seem to think The Box was created to annoy you personally. The Army hasn't the technical knowledge to destroy it, but it has sense enough to realize that more than just New York is under attack here. The enemy, whoever he may be, thinks his screen uncrackable, otherwise he wouldn't have given us this chance to work on it by boxing in one city alone. If The Box is not down in, say, eight days, he'll know that New York failed and died – and every city in the country will be bombed to slag the next morning."

Schafer sat down again, looking surly. "Why?" he asked the army man. "Why would they waste the bombs when they could just box in the cities?"

"Inefficient. America's too big to occupy except slowly, piecemeal. They'd have no reason to care if large parts of it were uninhabitable for a while. The important thing is to knock us out as a military force, as a power in world affairs."

"If they boxed in all the cities at once — "

The colonel shook his head. "We have rocket emplacements of our own, and they *aren't* in large cities. Neither Box not bomb would catch more than a few of them. No. They have to know that The Box is uncrackable, so they can screen their own cities against our bombs until our whole country is knocked out. With The Box, that would take more than a week, and their cities would suffer along with ours. With bombs, a day would be enough. So they've allowed us this test. If New York comes out of this, there'll be no attack, at least until they've gotten a better screen. The Box seems good enough so far!"

"Politics," Schafer said, shaking his head disgustedly. "It's much too devious for me! Doesn't The Box constitute an attack?"

"Certainly – but who's doing the attacking?" the colonel demanded. "We can guess, but we don't know. And I doubt very much that the enemy has left any traces."

Meister stiffened suddenly, a thrill of astonishment shooting up his backbone. Schafer stared at him.

"Traces!" Meister said. "Of course! That is what has been stopping us all along. Naturally there would be no traces. We have been wasting time looking for them. Frank, the

91

generator is not in the Empire State Building. *It is not even in The Box!"*

"But, Jake, it's got to be," Schafer said. "It's physically impossible for it to be outside!"

"A trick," Dean rumbled.

Meister waved his hands excitedly. "No, no! This is the reasoning which has made our work so fruitless. Observe. As the colonel says, the enemy would not dare leave traces. Now, workmanship is traceable, particularly if the device is revolutionary, as this one is. Find that generator and you know at once which country has made it. You observe the principle, and you say to yourself, 'Ah, yes, there were reports, rumors, whispers of shadows of rumors of such a principle, but I discounted them as fantasy; they came out of Country X.' Do you follow?"

"Yes, but — "

"But no country would leave such a fingerprint where it could be found. This we can count upon. Whereas we know as yet next to nothing about the physics of The Box. Therefore, if it is physically impossible for the generator to be outside The Box, this does not mean that we must continue to search for it inside. It means that we must find a physical principle which makes it possible to be outside!"

Frank Schafer threw up his hands. "Revise basic physics in a week! Well, let's try. I suppose Meister's allowed lab work, Colonel?"

"Certainly, as long as my guards aren't barred from the laboratory."

Thirty hours later the snow stopped falling, leaving a layer a little over three inches deep. The battling mobs were no longer on the streets. Hopeless masses were jammed body to body in railroad stations and subways. The advancing ozone had driven the people in upon themselves, and into the houses and basements where rooms could be sealed against the searing stench.

Thousands had already died along the periphery. The

New Jersey and Brooklyn shores were charnel heaps of those who had fought to get back across the river to Manhattan and cleaner air. The tenements along the West Side of the island still blazed, – twenty linear blocks of them, – but the fire had failed to jump Ninth Avenue and was dying for want of fuel. Elsewhere it was very cold. The city was dying.

Over it, The Box was invisible. It was the third night.

In the big lab at the Team Office, Meister, Schafer, and the two technicians suddenly disappeared under a little Box of their own, leaving behind four frantic soldiers. Meister sighed gustily and looked at the black screen a few feet from his head.

"Now we know," he said. "Frank, you can turn on the light now."

The desk lamp clicked on. In the shaded glow Meister saw that tears were trickling down Schafer's cheeks.

"No, no, don't weep yet, the job is not quite done!" Meister cried. "But see – so simple, so beautiful!" He gestured at the lump of metal in the exact center of the Boxed area. "Here we are – four men, a bit of metallic trash, an empty desk, a lamp, a cup of foil. Where is the screen generator? Outside!"

Schafer swallowed. "But it isn't," he said hoarsely. "Oh, you were right, Jake – the key projector *is* outside. But it doesn't generate the screen; it just excites the iron there, and that does the job." He looked at the scattered graphs on the desk top. "I'd never have dreamed such a jam of fields was possible! Look at those waves – catching each other, heterodyning, slowing each other up as the tension increases. No wonder the whole structure of space gives way when they finally get in phase!"

One of the technicians looked nervously at the little Box and cleared his throat. "I still don't see why it should leak light, oxygen, and so forth, even the little that it does. The jam has to be radiated away, and the screen should be the subspatial equivalent of a perfect radiator, a black body: But it's gray."

"No, it's black," Schafer said. "But it isn't turned on all the time. If it were, the catalyst radiation couldn't get through. It's a perfect electromagnetic push-me-pull-you. The apparatus outside projects the catalyst fields in. The lump of iron – in this case the Empire State Building – is excited and throws off the screen fields. The screen goes up. The screen cuts off the catalyst radiation. The screen goes down. In comes the primary beam again. And so on. The kicker is that without the off-again-on-again, you wouldn't get anything – the screen couldn't exist because the intermittence supplies some of the necessary harmonics."

He grinned ruefully. "Here I am explaining it as if I understood it. You're a good teacher, Jake!"

"Once one realizes that the screen has to *be* up before it can *go* up," Meister said, grinning back, "one has the rest – or most of it. Introducing a rhythmic interruption of the very first pulses is a simple trick. The hardest thing about it is timing – to know just when the screen goes up for the first time, so that the blinker can be cut out at precisely that moment."

"So how do we get out?"

"Feedback," Meister said. "There must be an enormous back EMF in the incoming beam. And whether it is converted and put back into the system again at the source, or just efficiently wasted, we can burn it out." He consulted a chalk line which ran along the floor from the edge of the little Box to the lump of iron, then picked up the cup of foil and pointed it along the mark away from the lump. "The trick," he said soberly, "is not to nullify, but to amplify — "

The glare of the overheads burst in upon them. The lab was jammed with soldiers, all with rifles at the ready and all the rifles pointing in at them. The smell of burned insulation curled from an apparatus at the other end of the chalk line.

"Oh," said Schafer. "We forgot the most important thing! Which way does our chalk line run from the Empire State Building, I wonder?"

"It could be anywhere above the horizon," Meister said. "Try pointing your reflector straight up, first."

Schafer swore. "Anytime you want a diploma for unscrewing the inscrutable, Jake," he said, "I'll write you one with my nose!"

It was cold and quiet now in the city. The fires on the West Side, where one of the country's worst slums had been burned out, smoldered and flickered.

The air was a slow, cumulative poison. It was very dark.

On top of the Empire State Building a great, shining bowl swung in a certain direction, stopped, waited. Fifty miles above it, in a region where neither *cold* nor *air* have any human meaning, a clumsy torpedo began to warm slightly. Inside it, delicate things glowed, fused – melted. There was no other difference; the torpedo kept on, traveled at its assigned twenty-one and eight-tenths miles per minute. It would always do so.

The Box vanished. The morning sunlight glared in. There was a torrent of rain as cold air hit hot July. Within minutes the city was as gray as before, but with roiling thunderheads. People poured out of the buildings into the downpour, hysterical faces turned to the free air, shouting amid the thunder, embracing each other, dancing in the lightning flares.

The storm passed almost at once, but the dancing went on quite a while.

"Traces!" Meister said to Frank Schafer. "Where else could you hide them? An orbital missile was the only answer."

"That sunlight," Schafer said, "sure looks good! You'd better go home to bed, Jake, before the official hero-worshipers catch up with you."

But Meister was already dreamlessly asleep.

Writing of the Rat

They had strapped the Enemy to a chair, which in John Jahnke's opinion was neither necessary nor smart, but Jahnke was only a captain (Field rank). Ugly the squat, gray-furred, sharp-toothed creatures were, certainly, and their thick bodies, well over six feet tall, were frighteningly strong. But they were also proud and intelligent. They never ran amok in a hopeless situation; that would be beneath their dignity.

The irons were going to make questioning the creature a good deal more difficult than it would have been otherwise – and that would have been difficult enough. But Jahnke was only a Field officer and, what was worse, invalided Home. Here it could hardly matter that he knew the Enemy better than any other human being alive. His opinions would be weighed against the fact that he had been invalided Home from a Field where there were no battles. And the two years of captivity? A rest cure, the Home officers called them.

"Where did you take him?" he asked Major Matthews.

"Off a planet of 31 Cygni," Mathews growled, loosening his tie. "Whopping sun, a hundred fifty times as big as Sol, six hundred fifty light-years from here. All alone there in a ship no bigger than himself."

"A scout?"

"What else? All right, he's ready." Matthews looked at the two hard-faced enlisted men behind the Enemy's chair. One of them grinned slightly. "Ask him where he's from."

97

The gray creature turned flat steady eyes on Jahnke, obviously already aware that he was the interpreter. Sweating, Jahnke put the question.

"Hnimesacpeo," the Enemy said.

"So far, so good," Jahnke murmured hopefully. "Hnimesacpeo *tce rebo?*"

"*Tca.*"

"Well?" Matthews demanded.

"That's the big province in the northern hemisphere of Vega III. Thus far, he's willing to be reasonable."

"The hell with that. We already knew he was Vegan. Where's his station?"

Whether or not the Enemy was Vegan was unknown and might never be known. But there was no point in arguing that with Matthews; he already thought he knew. After a moment's struggle with the language, Jahnke tried: "*Sftir etminbi rokolny?*"

"*R-daee blk.*"

"Either he doesn't understand me," Jahnke said resignedly, "or he won't talk while he's in the chair. He says, 'I just told you.'"

"Try again."

"*Dirafy edic,*" Jahnke said. "*Stfir etminbu rakolna?*"

"Hnimesacpeo." The creature's eyes blinked once. "*Ta hter o alkbee.*"

"It's no good," Jahnke said. "He's giving me the same answer, but this time in the pejorative form – the one they use for draft animals and children. It might go better if you'd let him out of those irons."

Matthews laughed shortly. "Tell him to open up or expect trouble. The irons are only the beginning."

"Sir, if you insist upon this course of action, I will appeal against it. It won't work and it's counter to policy. We know from long experience Outside that — "

"Never mind about Outside; you're on Earth now," Matthews retorted harshly. "Tell him what I said."

Worse and worse. Jahnke put the message as gently as he could.

The Enemy blinked. "*Sehe et broe in icen.*"

"Well?" Matthews snapped.

"He says you couldn't run a maze with your shoes off," Jahnke said, with grim relish. The phrase was *the* mortal insult, but Matthews wouldn't know that; the literal translation could mean little to him.

Nevertheless, Matthews had brains enough to know when he was being defied. He flushed furiously. "All right!" he told the toughs. "Start on him – and don't start slow!"

Jahnke was abruptly wishing that he hadn't translated the insult at all, but the outcome would probably have been the same in the long run. "Sir," he said, his voice ragged, "I request your permission to leave."

"Don't be stupid. Do you think we're doing this for fun?" Since this what exactly what Jahnke thought, he was glad that the question was rhetorical. "Who'll translate when he does talk, if you're not here?"

"He won't talk."

"Yes, he will," Matthews promised savagely. "And you can tell him why."

After a moment, Jahnke said stonily: "*Ocro hli antsoutinys, fuso tizen et tobee.*"

It was a complex message and Jahnke was none too sure that he had got it right. The Enemy merely nodded once and looked away. There was no way of telling whether he had failed to understand, had understood and was trying to avoid betraying Jahnke, or was merely indifferent. He said: "*Seace tce ctisbe.*" The phrase was formal; it might mean "thank you," but then again it might mean half a hundred equally common expressions, including "hello," "good-by," and "time for lunch."

"Does he understand?" Matthews demanded.

"I think he does," Jahnke said. "You'll be destroying him for nothing, Major."

99

Two hours later, the gray creature looked at Matthews out of his remaining, lidless eye, said clearly, "*Sehe et broe in icen,*" and died. He had said nothing else, though he had cried out often.

Somehow, that possible word of thanks he had given Jahnke made it worse, not better.

Jahnke went back to his quarters on shaky legs, to compose a letter of protest. He gave it up after the first paragraph. There was nobody to write to. While he had been Outside, he could have appealed to the Chief of Intelligence Operations (Field), who had been his friend as well as his immediate superior. But now he was in New Washington, where the CIO(F) in his remote flagship swung less weight than Home officers as far down the chain of command as Major Matthews.

It hadn't always been like that. After the discovery of the Enemy, the Field officers had commanded is much instant respect at Home us Field officers always had; they were in the position of danger. But as it gradually became clear that there was going to be no war, that the Field officers were bringing home puzzles instead of victories, that the danger Outside was that of precipitating a battle rather than fighting one, the pendulum swung. Now Field officers treated the Enemy with respect and were despised for it – while the Home officers itched for the chance to show that they weren't soft on the Enemy.

Matthews had had one chance and would be itching for another.

Jahnke put down his pen and stared at the wall, feeling more than a little sick.

The gray creatures were, as it had turned out, everywhere. When the first interstellar ship had arrived in the Alpha Centauri system, there they were, running the two fertile planets from vast stony cities by means of an elaborate priesthood. The relatively infertile fourth planet they had organized as a tight autarchy of technicians, dominating

100

a high-energy economy of scarcity. They had garrisoned several other utterly barren Centaurian planets, for what was vaguely called "reasons of policy," meaning that nobody knew why they had.

That had been only a foretaste. No habitable planet was without them, however far you stretched the definition of "habitable." Their most magnificent achievement was Vega III, an Earthlike world twice the diameter of Earth and at least a century in advance of Earth technologies. But they were found, too, on the major satellite of 61 Cygni C, a "gray ghost" star almost small enough to be a gas-giant planet, where they lived tribal lives as cramped and penurious as those of ancient Lapland – and had the Ragnarok-like mythology to go with it.

No one could even guess how long they had known interstellar flight or where they had come from. The hypothesis that they had originally been Vegans was shaky, based solely on the fact that Vega III was their most highly developed planet yet discovered. As for facts that argued in the opposite direction, there were more than enough, from Jahnke's point of view.

They had, for instance, a common spoken language, but every one of their civilizations had a different written language, usually irreconcilable with all the others – pictograms, phonetic systems, ideograms, hieratic short-hands, inflectional systems, tone-modulated systems, positional systems – the works. The spoken language was so complex that not even Jahnke could speak it above primer level, for it was based on phoneme placement inside the word. In short, it was totally synthetic, derived from the Enemy's vast knowledge of information theory, and could be matched up *in part* to any written language imaginable.

Thus there was no way to tell what written language – which always abstracts from speech and introduces new elements that have nothing to do with speech – might have been the original.

*   *   *

101

And how can you be sure you know where the Enemy's home planet is, Jahnke brooded, when you can see him still actively exploring and taking over one new system after another, for no other visible reason than sheer acquisitiveness? How can you tell how long that process has been going on, when *no* new penetration of human beings to more distant reaches of the Galaxy fails to find the gray creatures established on two or three promising planets, and nosing in on half a dozen additional cinder-blocks which have nothing to recommend them but the fact that they are large enough to land upon?

"They're nothing but six-foot-tall rats," Col. Singh, the CIO(F), had once told Jahnke, in a tone of disgust unusual for him. "The whole damned Galaxy must be overrun with them. They couldn't have evolved any civilization we ever found them in."

"They're intelligent," Jahnke had protested. "Nobody's yet measured how intelligent they are."

"Sure," Singh had said. "I'll give them that much credit. They're more than intelligent – they're brilliant. Nevertheless they didn't evolve any of 'their' civilizations, John. They couldn't have, because the civilizations are too diversified. The Enemy maintains all of them with equal thoroughness and equal indifference. If we could just explore some of those planets, I'll bet we'd find the bones of the original owners. How does that poem of Pound's go?"

His brow furrowed a moment over this apparent irrelevancy and he quoted:

> "*And the wind shifts*
> *and the dust on a doorsill shifts*
> *and even the writing of the rat footprints*
> *tells us nothing, nothing at all*
> *about the greatest city, the greatest nation*
> *where the strong men listened*
> *and the women warbled:*
> *Nothing like us ever was.*"

"That's how it is," Sing added gloomily. "All these gray rats are doing is picking everybody else's cupboards. They're very good at that. They may well be picking ours before long."

That was the second theory; on the whole, it was the most popular one now. It was the theory under which a man like Matthews could torture to death a creature several times as intelligent as he was and with a code of customs and a set of moral standards which made Matthews look like a bushman, on the grounds that the Enemy were merely loathsome scavengers, fit only for extermination.

Despite his respect for Piara Singh, Jahnke could find little good to say for the rat theory, either. Both theories pointed, in the end, toward a common military goal – that of finding the Enemy's home planet and destroying it. If Vega III was the Enemy's home, then at least there was a target. If the Enemy were spreading from some other heartland, then the target still remained to be found.

But what good was that? It was military nonsense. The Enemy outnumbered humanity by millions to one. On the highly developed planets like Vega III, the Enemy commanded weapons compared to which humanity's best were only torches to be waved in the face of the inevitable night. The first moment of open warfare would be the end of humanity.

So far, the gray creatures and humanity were not at war. But the time of the explosion was drawing closer. Jahnke did not really think that the Enemy could be still in ignorance of Earth's practice of picking up its lone scouts for questioning; the Enemy's resources were too great.

It was his private theory, shared by Piara Singh, that the Enemy was content to let its scouts be questioned, as long as they were set free unharmed later. After all, the Enemy had once picked up Jahnke under the same circumstances and for that same purpose. It was for that reason that he knew their language better than any other human being; he had lived among them for two years.

But if Matthew's Inquisition methods represented a new and general policy toward these occasional captives, the Enemy would not let that policy go unprotested. The gray creatures were very proud. Jahnke knew that, for they had expected no less pride of him.

And what would happen when one of the Enemy's scouts came nosing, at long last, into the Solar System of Earth – even around so cold, dark and useless a world as the satellite of Proserpine, far beyond Pluto? Earth had no use for that rockball, but it would never let the "rats" have it, just the same. The gray tide had spared the Sol system, but that couldn't last forever. It had spared nothing else.

The phone rang insistently, jarring Jahnke out of his bitter reverie. He picked it up.

"Captain Jahnke? One moment, please. Colonel Singh calling."

Jahnke clung to the phone in a state of numb shock, uncertain whether to be delighted or appalled. What could Piara Singh be doing here, out of the high free emptiness of Outside? Had he been invalided Home again, too, or had some failure —

"John? How are you? This is Singh; I called the moment I got in."

"Hello, Colonel. I'm astonished and pleased. But what—"

"I know what you're thinking," the CIO(F) said rapidly. His voice was high with suppressed eagerness; Jahnke had never heard him sound so young before. "I'm Home on my own initiative, on special orders I wormed out of old Wu himself. I brought a prisoner with me. John, listen, he's the most important prisoner we've ever taken. *He told me his name!*"

"No! They never do! It's against the rules!"

"But he did," Singh said, almost bubbling. "It's Hrestce. In the language, it means 'compromise,' isn't that right? I

104

think he was deliberately sent to us with a message. That's why I came Home. The key to the whole problem seems to be in his hands and he obviously wants to talk. I have to have you to listen to him and tell me what it means."

Jahnke's heart tried to rise and sink at the same time, enclosing his whole chest in an awful vise of apprehension. "All right," he said faintly. "Did you notify CIO? Here in New Washington, I mean?"

"Oh, of course." Singh's enthusiasm seemed to be about to burst the telephone handset – and small wonder, after all the setbacks that had made up his career Outside. "They recognized right away how important this is. They've assigned their best interrogation man to me, a Major Matthews. I don't doubt that he's good, but we'll need you first. If you can get here for a preliminary talk with Hrestce — "

"I can get there," Jahnke said tensely. "But don't let *anyone* else talk to him before I do. This Matthews is dangerous; if he phones before I arrive, stall him. Where are you calling from?"

"At home on the Kattegat. I have three weeks' leave. You know the place, don't you? You can reach it in an hour, if you can catch a rocket immediately. I can keep Hrestce in my jurisdiction for you that long easily. Nobody but you and the CIO knows he's here."

"Don't even let CIO at him until I get there. I'll see you in an hour."

"Right, John. Good-by."

"*Seace tce ctisbe.*"

"Yes – how does it go? *Tca.*"

"*Tce; tca.*"

Trembling with excitement and urgency, Jahnke got the rest of his mussed uniform off, clambered into mufti and packed his equipment: a tape recorder, two dictionaries compiled by himself, a set of frequency tables for the Enemy language which he had not yet completed, and a toothbrush. At the last moment, he remembered to take his officer's ID card and money to buy his rocket ticket. Now. All ready.

He opened the door to go out.

Matthews was there. His feet were wide apart, his hands locked behind his back, his face thrust forward. He looked like a lowering, small-scale copy of the Colossus of Rhodes.

"Morning, Captain Jahnke," Matthews said, with a slight and nasty smile. "Going somewhere? The Kattegat, maybe?"

The soldiers behind Matthews, those same two wooden-faced toughs, helped him wait for Jahnke's answer.

After a moment of sickening doubt, Jahnke retreated into his quarters, to the kitchen, out of Matthew's sight. He found the bottle of cloudy ammonia his batman used for scrubbing his floors and shook it until it was full of foam. Then he went back to the front room and threw the bottle as hard as he could into the corridor. It seemed to explode like a bomb.

He had to knee one soldier who clawed through the fumes into the front room; he got away over the man's writhing body. His eyes were streaming. Now he had to reach Singh before Matthews did.

It would be a near thing. Temporarily, at least, time was on his side, Jahnke was pretty sure. Piara Singh's Kattegat home was a retreat, quite possibly unlisted among the addresses the government had for him; Jahnke had learned of it only through a few moments of nostalgia in which the colonel had indulged over a drink. If so, Matthews would have a difficult time searching the shores of the strait for it, and might think only very belatedly of looking in the wildest part of Jutland.

Also in Jahnke's favor was the fact that Matthews was only a major. The man whose leave he had to plan on invading was a full colonel, even though only a despised Field officer – and the scorn in which Field officers were held was in itself only a symptom of the Home officers' guilt

106

at being Home officers. Matthews would probably pause to collect considerable official backing before venturing further.

All this was logical, but Jahnke knew Matthews too well to be comforted by it.

He got a liner direct to Copenhagen, which cut down his transit time considerably. After that, there was only the complicated business of getting off the islands onto the peninsula, and thence north to Alborg. Col. Singh had a car waiting for him there, which took him direct to the lodge.

"An hour and a half," Singh said, shaking hands. "That was good time."

"Glad to see you, sir. We're going to have to move fast, I'm afraid; we're not safe even here. This Matthews is a dedicated sadist. Do you remember the prisoner that was sent home with me? Well, Matthews tortured him to death yesterday, trying to get routine information out of him. He'll do the same with your captive if he gets his hands on him. He knows I'm here, of course. Either my telephone wire was tapped or he knew that you'd call me as soon as the news trickled down to him at CIO."

An expression of revulsion totally transformed Col. Singh's lean brown face for a moment, but he said decisively: "So it's come to that; they must be cut off from the real situation Outside almost entirely, and it's their own fault. Well, I know what we can do. I have a private plane here and my pilot is the very best. We'll just take ourselves upstairs and defy this Matthews to get us down until we're ready."

"Where are we going?" Jahnke asked.

"I don't know at the moment and it doesn't matter. There are a lot of places to hide inside a thousand-mile radius where Matthews wouldn't think of looking for us, if we *have* to hide. But I think I can pull his teeth through channels before it comes to that. Come on, better meet the prisoner."

He led the way into the next room. The prisoner was

107

looking at a book which, Jahnke could see as he put it aside, was mostly mathematics. He was an unusually big specimen even for an Enemy, almost seven feet tall, with enormous shoulders and arms, a deep chest, and a brow which gave him an expression of permanent ferocity. He looked as though he could have torn Jahnke and the colonel to pieces without the slightest effort, as indeed he probably could.

"Hrestce, John Jahnke," Col. Singh said.

"*Seace tce ctisbe*," Jahnke said.

"*Tca*." Hrestce held out his hand and Jahnke took it, somewhat nervously. Then, drawing a deep breath, he quickly outlined the situation, pulling no punches. When he got to the part about the death of Matthews' prisoner, Hrestce only nodded; when Jahnke proposed that they leave, he nodded again. That was all.

In the cabin of the plane, Jahnke started his tape recorder and got out his manuscript dictionary. With Hrestce's first words, however, it became apparent that he wasn't going to need the dictionary. The Enemy spoke simply, though with great dignity, and quickly found the speechrate which was comfortable for Jahnke. When he spoke to Singh, he slowed down even more; he seemed already aware that Singh's command of the language did not extend to high-order abstractions or subtle constructions.

"I am an emissary, as Colonel Singh surmised," Hrestce said. "My mission is to apprise you of the search my people have been conducting and to take such further steps as your reaction dictates. By 'you,' of course, I mean mankind."

"What is the search?" Jahnke inquired.

"First I must explain some other matters," Hrestce said. "You have some incomplete truths about us which should be completed right now. You know that we occupy many dissimilar civilisations; you suspect that they are not ours and that the original owners are gone. That is true. You think you have never seen our home culture. That is also

108

true; our planet of origin is far out on the end of this spiral arm of the Galaxy, from which we have been working our way inward toward the center. You think we have usurped the original owners of these cultures. That is not true. We have another function. We are custodians."

"Custodians?" Singh repeated.

"Of cultures, of entire ecologies. That is the role which has been thrust upon us. When we first mastered interstellar flight, sometime in the prehistory of your race, we found these abandoned planets by the hundreds. We found only a few inhabited ones, which I will describe in a moment.

"The research that followed was tedious and I shall do no more than describe its results. Briefly, there is a race in the Galaxy *which is practicing slavery upon an incredible scale*. We know who they are, for we have encountered several of their slave-planets, but they fight ferociously and without quarter, so that we have been unable to find out where they came from, or why they want so many billions and billions of slaves. Their usual practice, however, is to evacuate a planet entirely; there is evidence of resistance on all the empty worlds, but the battles and losses were never large – evidently the slavers utterly overwhelmed them. The bones we find never account for more than a tenth of the total population of the planet, usually much less. Yet the people are gone, leaving nothing behind but their effects, which the raiders seldom bother to loot.

"We do not know how many of these conquered and enslaved races are still alive. Under the circumstances, we have chosen to maintain each culture on its own terms, in the hope that at least some of them may be repossessed by their owners in the future, as we have already turned back the liberated worlds. It is for that reason that we have evolved this synthetic language, which is adaptable to any culture and carries the implicit assumptions of none."

The gray creature paused and the expression which crossed his face was something like a fleeting smile. "After speaking it for so many millennia, we find we rather like it. Some of us are doing creative work in it."

"I like it very well," Jahnke said. "It's highly flexible; I should think it might make a good medium for poetry."

"There you make a statement with import for your race." The smile, if that was what it had been, was gone without a trace. "It was your captivity, to some extent, that deterred us from wiping you all out at once, as we have the power to do. For I must tell you plainly now that *you are an outpost of the slavers we are seeking.*"

Jahnke had seen it coming, if only hazily; but it hurt, all the same.

"We were in doubt at first. Though the physical form is the same, your obvious creativity and your frequent flashes of sanity and decency seemed anomalous. Also, there seemed to be evidence that you had evolved on this planet. Further investigation disposed of that point, however; of all your presumptive ancestors, only the extinct half-simian, stone-throwing culture of South Africa is indigenous to Earth. All the others, plus many forms that puzzle your naturalists, you brought with you from other planets – as slaves or food – and the stone-throwers you wiped out as being of too little intelligence to be useful. The Cro-Magnons, for example, were the descendants of the race of Vega III; there is no doubt whatever about it."

Jahnke asked hollowly: "What now? Since you have decided not to wipe us out — "

"There is the heart of the question," Hrestce said. "You have been cut off a long time from the moral monsters who spawned you and during that time you have changed. Your race still reverts to the parent type now and then: you produce an Alexander, a Khan, a Napoleon, a Hitler, a Stalin, a MacHinery – or a Matthews. But plainly, these are now sub-human types and will become even more rare with time.

"We have been hunting for the main body of these slavers

110

for a long time. They have crimes beyond number to answer for. They may have changed greatly in twenty-five thousand years, as you have changed; if so, we will be gratified. If they have not changed, we are prepared to destroy them down to the last monster."

Hrestce paused and looked at the two men with somber ferocity.

"The task is enormous," he said, "because of the care-taking responsibilities that go with it. We would share it with someone if we could. We have decided to ask you if you would agree to to share it. The growth you have undergone is staggering; it shows potentialities which we believe are greater than ours."

A long sigh exploded from Singh; evidently he had been holding his breath longer than he himself had realized. "So all the time *you* were the rat-terriers and *we* were the rats. Matthews fits the description, all right. When I get through with him, he's going to be breaking rocks."

As for Jahnke, he would have found it hard to say whether he was awed or elated, for both emotions had overwhelmed him at once. Matthews and his breed were certainly through; the Field officers had brought home not only the bacon, but the laurel wreath – not a bloody victory to be lived down, but a mighty standard to be followed.

"Can we accept?" Jahnke breathed at last.

The colonel stood shakily and went forward to the door of the control cubby. "West as she goes," he told the pilot huskily. "For New Washington. And get me the Secretary-General on the radio."

"Yes, sir."

Piara Singh closed the door and came back. While the plane turned over the dark Atlantic, the three rat-terriers put their heads together.

In some cupboard toward the center of the Galaxy, the writing of the rat was waiting to be read.

A Matter of Energy

As soon as I saw Joe Jones, I knew that he was the man I needed to send back to the Augustan Age. I knew it because I could not read his expression.

To the ordinary man who can't even read his own expression this wouldn't be a significant datum, but with me it is different. As a consulting industrial psionic psichologist I am accustomed to reading the faces of anything, even checks. I always understand everybody instantly.

But I didn't understand Joe Jones. He was Everyman's nobody. He had no emotions. If he had had them, I could have read them – if not by the patterns formed by the hairs in his moustache, then by the psionic techniques which I have developed by correspondence with psichotic people all over the country. So it had to be true that Joe had no emotions.

He was the perfect man to go back in time and take over the Augustan Age for me.

"Joe," I asseverated, "I've given you the invincible weapon to take over the Romans: twisted semantics. It can't fail, but if it does, try twisted dianetics. Do you understand what you're to do?"

"Yes, Cliff," he lipped thinly.

"But there's one danger I haven't warned you of until now," I admonished sternly. "You must not use Arabic numerals while you're in Rome. The Romans didn't know them. If you use them you will be driven to hide like a witch. Understand?"

"Yes, Cliff," he acknowledged flatly.

"Now, I haven't given you any training in how to calculate in Roman numerals," I outpointed. "I could have given it to you by my own revolutionary educational system, or implanted it on your cerebral cortex with my psionic powers, but there's one great drawback: calculating with Roman numerals just takes too long. You wouldn't have time to take over the Empire if you had to do all your figuring that way. Is that clear?"

"That's clear, Cliff," he admitted immediately.

"So," I perorated triumphantly. "I've provided you with the answer, inside this little black box. This is a computer, called the THROBAC. That's short for *TH*rifty *RO*man-numeral *BA*ckwards-looking *C*alculator. It will add, subtract, multiply or divide in Roman numerals, and give you the answer in Roman numerals. Coupling and that crowd at Bell think that they invented it, but I can see through *them* like a glass of antigravity elixir. Use this machine – secretly, of course – whenever you need to do any figuring. Do you dig me?"

"I dig you, Cliff," he penultimated.

"Then go," I concluded commandingly. He stepped into the time machine, which I had named ELSIE, and vanished at once. With the help of my psionic correspondents I could have sent him back without a machine, but this whole operation had to be kept secret from the politicians, industrialists, and other pressure groups who might bring twisted semantics to bear on me.

He was back in no time, of course. He had instructions to return to this moment, no matter how long he stayed in ancient Rome. But there was something wrong.

I could read his expression!

"What have you done?" I hissed grindingly.

"I did just like you said, Cliff," he replied defensively. "Soon as I had to do some figuring, I holed up in my room and plugged THROBAC into the nearest socket. But — "

"Get to the point!" I ordered commandingly.

114

"But, Cliff," he wailed protestingly, "you overlooked something. THROBAC operates only on AC current! And the first AC generator wasn't built until after the 1830s – A.D.!"

I was crushed. That small oversight – no, it was an undersight, typical of me, underestimating the extent of my own massive knowledge – must have blown every fuse and circuit-breaker in Augustan Rome. I rushed to the nearest history book.

What had I undone?

King of the Hill

It did Col. Hal Gascoigne no good whatsoever to know that he was the only man aboard Satellite Vehicle 1. No good at all. He had stopped reminding himself of the fact some time back.

And now, as he sat sweating in the perfectly balanced air in front of the bombardier board, one of the men spoke to him again:

"Colonel, sir — "

Gascoigne swung around in the seat, and the sergeant – Gascoigne could almost remember the man's name – threw him a snappy Air Force salute.

"Well?"

"Bomb one is primed, sir. Your orders?"

"My orders?" Gascoigne said wonderingly. But the man was already gone. Gascoigne couldn't actually *see* the sergeant leave the control cabin, but he was no longer in it.

While he tried to remember, another voice rang in the cabin, as flat and razzy as all voices sound on an intercom.

"Radar room. On target."

A regular, meaningless peeping. The timing circuit had cut in.

Or had it? There was nobody in the radar room. There was nobody in the bomb hold, either. There had never been anybody on board SV-1 but Gascoigne, not since he had relieved Grinnell – and Grinnell had flown the station up here in the first place.

Then who had that sergeant been? His name was . . . It was . . .

The hammering of the teletype blanked it out. The noise was as loud as a pom-pom in the echoing metal cave. He got up and coasted across the deck to the machine, gliding in the gravity-free cabin with the ease of a man to whom free fall is almost second nature.

The teletype was silent by the time he reached it, and at first the tape looked blank. He wiped the sweat out of his eyes. There was the message.

MNBVCXZ LKJ HGFDS PYTR AOIU EUIO QPALZM

He got out his copy of *The Well-Tempered Pogo* and checked the speeches of Grundoon the Beaver-Chile for the key letter-sequence on which the code was based. There weren't very many choices. He had the clear in ten minutes.

BOMB ONE WASHINGTON 1700 HRS TAMMANANY

There it was. That was what he had been priming the bomb for. But there should have been earlier orders, giving him the go-ahead to prime. He began to rewind the paper.

It was all blank.

And – *Washington?* Why would the Joint Chiefs of Staff order him —

"Colonel Gascoigne, sir."

Gascoigne jerked around and returned the salute. "What's your name?" he snapped.

"Sweeney, sir," the corporal said. Actually it didn't sound very much like Sweeney, or like anything else; it was just a noise. Yet the man's face looked familiar. "Ready with bomb two, sir."

The corporal saluted, turned, took two steps, and faded. He did not vanish, but he did not go out the door, either. He simply receded, became darker and harder to distinguish, and was no longer there. It was as though he and Gascoigne had disagreed about the effects of perspective in the glowing Earthlight, and Gascoigne had turned out to be wrong.

Numbly, he finished rewinding the paper. There was no doubt about it. There the order stood, black on yellow, as plain as plain. Bomb the capital of your own country at 1700 hours. Just incidentally, bomb your own home in the process, but don't give that a second thought. Be thorough, drop two bombs; don't worry about missing by a few seconds of arc and hitting Baltimore instead, or Silver Spring, or Milford, Del. CIG will give you the coordinates, but plaster the area anyhow. That's S.O.P.

With rubbery fingers, Gascoigne began to work the keys of the teletype. Sending on the frequency of Civilian Intelligence Group, he typed:

HELP SHOUT SERIOUS REPEAT SERIOUS PERSONNEL TROUBLE HERE STOP DON'T KNOW HOW LONG I CAN KEEP IT DOWN STOP URGENT GASCOIGNE SV ONE STOP

Behind him, the oscillator peeped rhythmically, timing the drive on the launching rack trunnion.

"Radar room. On target."

Gascoigne did not turn. He sat before the bombardier board and sweated in the perfectly balanced air. Inside his skull, his own voice was shouting:

STOP STOP STOP

That, as we reconstructed it afterwards, is how the SV-1 affair began. It was pure luck, I suppose, that Gascoigne sent his message direct to us. Civilian Intelligence Group is rarely called into an emergency when the emergency is just being born. Usually Washington tries to do the bailing job first. Then, when Washington discovers that the boat is still sinking, it passes the bailing can to us – usually with a demand that we transform it into a centrifugal pump, on the double.

We don't mind. Washington's failure to develop a government department similar in function to CIG is the reason why we're in business. The profits, of course, go to Affiliated Enterprises, Inc., the loose corporation of universities and industries which put up the money to build

119

ULTIMAC – and ULTIMAC is, in turn, the reason why Washington comes running to CIG so often.

This time, however, it did not look like the big computer was going to be of much use to us. I said as much to Joan Hadamard, our social sciences division chief, when I handed her the message.

"Um," she said. "*Personnel* trouble? What does he mean? He hasn't got any personnel on that station."

This was no news to me. CIG provided the figures that got the SV-1 into its orbit in the first place, and it was on our advice that it carried only one man. The crew of a space vessel either has to be large or it has to be a lone man; there is no intermediate choice. And SV-1 wasn't big enough to carry a large crew – not to carry them and keep the men from flying at each other's throats sooner or later, that is.

"He means himself," I said. "That's why I don't think this is a job for the computer. It's going to have to be played person-to-person. It's my bet that the man's responsibility-happy; that danger was always implicit in the one-man recommendation."

"The only decent solution is a full complement," Joan agreed. "Once the Pentagon can get enough money from Congress to build a big station."

"What puzzles me is, why did he call us instead of his superiors?"

"That's easy. We process his figures. He trusts us. The Pentagon thinks we're infallible, and he's caught the disease from them."

"That's bad," I said.

"I've never denied it."

"No, what I mean is that it's bad that he called us instead of going through channels. It means that the emergency is at least as bad as he says it is."

I thought about it another precious moment longer while Joan did some quick dialing. As everybody on Earth – with the possible exception of a few Tibetans – already knew, the man who rode SV-1 rode with three hydrogen bombs

120

immediately under his feet – bombs which he could drop with great precision on any spot on the Earth. Gascoigne was, in effect, the sum total of American foreign policy; he might as well have had 'Spatial Supremacy' stamped on his forehead.

"What does the Air Force say?" I asked Joan as she hung up.

"They say they're a little worried about Gascoigne. He's a very stable man, but they had to let him run a month over his normal replacement time – why, they don't explain. He's been turning in badly garbled reports over the last week. They're thinking about giving him a dressing down."

"Thinking! They'd better be careful with that stuff, or they'll hurt themselves. Joan, somebody's going to have to go up there. I'll arrange fast transportation, and tell Gascoigne that help is coming. Who should go?"

"I don't have a recommendation," Joan said. "Better ask the computer."

I did so – on the double.

ULTIMAC said: *Harris.*

"Good luck, Peter," Joan said calmly. Too calmly.

"Yeah," I said. "Or good night."

Exactly what I expected to happen as the ferry rocket approached SV-1, I don't now recall. I had decided that I couldn't carry a squad with me. If Gascoigne was really far gone, he wouldn't allow a group of men to disembark; one man, on the other hand, he might pass. But I suppose I did expect him to put up an argument first.

Nothing happened. He did not challenge the ferry, and he didn't answer hails. Contact with the station was made through the radar automatics, and I was put off on board as routinely as though I was being let into a movie – but a lot more rapidly.

The control room was dark and confusing, and at first I didn't see Gascoigne anywhere. The Earthlight coming through the observation port was brilliant, but beyond the edges of its path the darkness was almost absolute, broken only by the little stars of indicator lenses.

A faint snicking sound turned my eyes in the right direction. There was Gascoigne. He was hunched over the bombardier board, his back to me. In one hand he held a small tool resembling a ticket punch. Its jaws were nibbling steadily at a taut line of tape running between two spools; that had been the sound I'd heard. I recognized the device without any trouble; it was a programmer.

But why hadn't Gascoigne heard me come in? I hadn't tried to sneak up on him, there is no quiet way to come through an air lock anyway. But the punch went on snicking steadily.

"Colonel Gascoigne," I said. There was no answer. I took a step forward. "Colonel Gascoigne, I'm Harris of CIG. What are you doing?"

The additional step did the trick. "Stay away from me," Gascoigne growled, from somewhere way down in his chest. "I'm programming the bomb. Punching in the orders myself. Can't depend on my crew. Stay away."

"Give over for a minute. I want to talk to you."

"That's a new one," said Gascoigne, not moving. "Most of you guys were rushing to set up launchings before you even reported to me. Who the hell are you, anyhow? There's nobody on board, I know *that* well enough."

"I'm Peter Harris," I said. "From CIG – you called us, remember? You asked us to send help."

"Doesn't prove a thing. Tell me something I *don't* know. Then maybe I'll believe you exist. Otherwise – beat it."

"Nothing doing. Put down that punch."

Gascoigne straightened slowly and turned to look at me. "Well, you don't vanish, I'll give you that," he said. "What did you say your name was?"

"Harris. Here's my ID card."

Gascoigne took the plastic-coated card tentatively, and then removed his glasses and polished them. The gesture itself was perfectly ordinary, and wouldn't have surprised me – except that Gascoigne was not wearing glasses.

"It's hard to see in here," he complained. "Everything gets so steamed up. Hm. All right, you're real. What do you want?"

His finger touched a journal. Silently, the tape began to roll from one spool to another.

"Gascoigne, stop that thing. If you drop any bombs there'll be hell to pay. It's tense enough down below as it is. And there's no reason to bomb anybody."

"Plenty of reason," Gascoigne muttered. He turned toward the teletype, exposing to me for the first time a hip holster cradling a large, black automatic. I didn't doubt that he could draw it with fabulous rapidity, and put the bullets just where he wanted them to go. "I've got orders. There they are. See for yourself."

Cautiously, I sidled over to the teletype and looked. Except for Gascoigne's own message to CIG, and one from Joan Hadamard announcing that I was on my way, the paper was totally blank. There had been no other messages that day unless Gascoigne had changed the roll, and there was no reason why he should have. Those rolls last close to forever.

"When did this order come in?"

"This morning some time. I don't know. Sweeney!" he bawled suddenly, so loud that the paper tore in my hands. "When did that drop order come through?"

Nobody answered. But Gascoigne said almost at once, "There, you heard him."

"I didn't hear anything but you," I said, "and I'm going to stop that tape. Stand aside."

"Not a chance, Mister," Gascoigne said grimly. "The tape rides."

"Who's getting hit?"

"Washington," Gascoigne said, and passed his hand over his face. He appeared to have forgotten the imaginary spectacles.

"That's where your home is, isn't it?"

"It sure is," Gascoigne said. "It sure as hell is, Mister. Cute, isn't it?"

It was cute, all right. The Air Force boys at the Pentagon were going to be given about ten milliseconds to be sorry they'd refused to send a replacement for Gascoigne along with me. *Replace him with who? We can't send his second alternate in anything short of a week. The man has to have retraining, and the first alternate's in the hospital with a ruptured spleen. Besides, Gascoigne's the best man for the job; he's got to be bailed out somehow.*

Sure. With a psychological centrifugal pump, no doubt. In the meantime the tape kept right on running.

"You might as well stop wiping your face, and turn down the humidity instead," I said. "You've already smudged your glasses again."

"Glasses?" Gascoigne muttered. He moved slowly across the cabin, sailing upright like a sea horse, to the blank glass of a closed port. I seriously doubted that he could see his reflection in it, but maybe he didn't really want to see it. "I messed them up, all right. Thanks." He went through the polishing routine again.

A man who thinks he is wearing glasses also thinks he can't see without them. I slid to the programmer and turned off the tape. I was between the spools and Gascoigne now – but I couldn't stay there forever.

"Let's talk a minute, Colonel," I said. "Surely it can't do any harm."

Gascoigne smiled, with a sort of childish craft. "I'll talk," he said. "Just as soon as you start that tape again. I was watching you in the mirror, *before* I took my glasses off."

The liar. I hadn't made a move while he'd been looking into that porthole. His poor pitiful weak old rheumy eyes had seen every move I made while he was polishing his "glasses." I shrugged and stepped away from the programmer.

124

"You start it," I said. "I won't take the responsibiltiy."

"It's orders," Gascoigne said woodenly. He started the tape running again. "It's their responsibility. What did you want to talk to me about, anyhow?"

"Colonel Gascoigne, have you ever killed anybody?"

He looked startled. "Yes, once I did," he said, almost eagerly. "I crashed a plane into a house. Killed the whole family. Walked away with nothing worse than a burned leg – good as new after a couple of muscle stabilizations. That's what made me shift from piloting to weapons; that leg's not quite good enough to fly with any more."

"Tough."

He snickered suddenly, explosively. "And now look at me," he said. "I'm going to kill my *own* family in a little while. And millions of other people. Maybe the whole world."

How long was "a little while"?

"What have you got against it?" I said.

"Against what – the world? Nothing. Not a damn thing. Look at me; I'm king of the hill up here. I can't complain."

He paused and licked his lips. "It was different when I was a kid," he said. "Not so dull, then. In those days you could get a real newspaper, that you could unfold for the first time yourself, and pick out what you wanted to read. Not like now, when the news comes to you predigested on a piece of paper out of your radio. That's what's the matter with it, if you ask me."

"What's the matter with what?"

"With the news – that's why it's always bad these days. Everything's had something done to it. The milk is homogenized, the bread is sliced, the cars steer themselves, the phonographs will produce sounds no musical instrument could make. Too much meddling, too many people who can't keep their hands off things. Ever fire a kiln?"

"Me?" I said, startled.

"No, I didn't think so. Nobody makes pottery these days.

125

Not by hand. And if they did, who'd buy it? They don't want something that's been made. They want something that's been Done To."

The tape kept on traveling. Down below, there was a heavy rumble, difficult to identify specifically: something heavy being shifted on tracks, or maybe a freight lock opening.

"So now you're going to Do Something to the Earth," I said slowly.

"Not me. It's orders."

"Orders from inside, Colonel Gascoigne. There's nothing on the spools." What else could I do? I didn't have time to take him through two years of psychoanalysis and bring him to his own insight. Besides, I'm not licensed to practice medicine – not on Earth. "I didn't want to say so, but I have to now."

"Say what?" Gascoigne said suspiciously. "That I'm crazy or something?"

"No. I didn't say that. You did," I pointed out. "But I will tell you that that stuff about not liking the world these days is baloney. Or rationalization, if you want a nicer word. You're carrying a screaming load of guilt, Colonel, whether you're aware of it or not."

"I don't know what you're talking about. Why don't you just beat it?"

"No. And you know well enough. You fell all over yourself to tell me about the family you killed in your flying accident." I gave him ten seconds of silence, and then shot the question at him as hard as I could. "*What was their name?*"

"How do I know? Sweeney or something. Anything. I don't remember."

"Sure you do. Do you think that killing your own family is going to bring the Sweeneys back to life?"

Gascoigne's mouth twisted, but he seemed to be entirely unaware of the grimace. "That's all hogwash," he said. "I never did hold with that psychological claptrap. It's you that's handing out the baloney, not me."

126

"Then why are you being so vituperative about it? Hogwash, claptrap, baloney – you are working awfully hard to knock it down, for a man who doesn't believe in it."

"Go away," he said sullenly. "I've got my orders. I'm obeying them."

Stalemate. But there was no such thing as stalemate up here. Defeat was the word.

The tape traveled. I did not know what to do. The last bomb problem CIG had tackled had been one we had set up ourselves; we had arranged for a dud to be dropped in New York harbour, to test our own facilities for speed in determining the nature of the missile. The situation on board SV-1 was completely different —

Whoa. Was it? Maybe I'd hit something there.

"Colonel Gascoigne," I said slowly, "you might as well know now that it isn't going to work. Not even if you do get that bomb off."

"Yes, I can. What's to stop me?" He hooked one thumb in his belt, just above the holster, so that his fingers tips rested on the breech of the automatic.

"Your bombs. They aren't alive."

Gascoigne laughed harshly and waved at the controls. "Tell that to the counter in the bomb hold. Go ahead. There's a meter you can read, right there on the bombardier board."

"Sure," I said. "The bombs are radioactive, all right. Have you ever checked their half life?"

It was a long shot. Gascoigne was a weapons man; if it were possible to check half life on board the SV-1, he would have checked it. But I didn't think it was possible.

"What would I do that for?"

"You wouldn't, being a loyal airman. You believe what your superiors tell you. But I'm a civilian, Colonel. There's no element in those bombs that will either fuse or fission. The half life is too long for tritium or for lithium 6, and it's too short for uranium 235 or radio-thorium. The stuff is probably strontium 90 – in short, nothing but a bluff."

"By the time I finished checking that," Gascoigne said, "the bomb would be launched anyhow. And you haven't checked it, either. Try another tack."

"I don't need to. You don't have to believe me. We'll just sit here and wait for the bomb drop, and then the point will prove itself. After that, of course, you'll be court-martialed for firing a wild shot without orders. But since you're prepared to wipe out your own family, you won't mind a little thing like twenty years in the guardhouse."

Gascoigne looked at the silently rolling tape. "Sure," he said, "I've got the orders, anyhow. The same thing would happen if I didn't obey them. If nobody gets hurt, so much the better."

A sudden spasm of emotion – I took it to be grief, but I could have been wrong – shook his whole frame for a moment. Again, he did not seem to notice it. I said:

"That's right. Not even your family. Of course the whole world will know the station's a bluff, but if those are the orders — "

"I don't know," Gascoigne said harshly. "I don't know whether I even got any orders. I don't remember where I put them. Maybe they're not real." He looked at me confusedly, and his expression was frighteningly like that of a small boy making a confession.

"You know something?" he said. "I don't know what's real any more. I haven't been able to tell, ever since yesterday. I don't even know if you are real, or your ID card either. What do you think of that?"

"Nothing," I said.

"Nothing! Nothing! That's my trouble. Nothing! I can't tell what's nothing and what's something. You say the bombs are duds. All right. But what if *you're* the dud, and the bombs are real? Answer me that!"

His expression was almost triumphant now.

"The bombs are duds," I said. "And you've gone and

steamed up your glasses again. Why don't you turn down the humidity, so you can see for three minutes hand running?"

Gascoigne leaned far forward, so far that he was perilously close to toppling, and peered directly into my face.

"Don't give me that," he said hoarsely. "Don't – give – me that – stuff."

I froze right where I was. Gascoigne watched my eyes for a while. Then, slowly, he put his hand on his forehead and began to wipe it downward. He smeared it over his face, in slow motion, all the way down to his chin.

Then he took the hand away and looked at it, as though it had just strangled him and he couldn't understand why. And finally he spoke.

"It – isn't true," he said dully. "I'm not wearing any glasses. Haven't worn glasses since I was ten. Not since I broke my last pair – playing King of the Hill."

He sat down before the bombardier board and put his head in his hands.

"You win," he said hoarsely. "I must be crazy as a loon. I don't know what I'm seeing and what I'm not. You better take this gun away. If I fired it I might even hit something."

"You're all right," I said. And I meant it; but I didn't waste any time all the same. The automatic first; then the tape. In that order, the sequence couldn't be reversed afterwards.

But the sound of the programmer's journal clicking to 'Off' was as loud in that cabin as any gunshot.

"He'll be all right," I told Joan afterwards. "He pulled himself through. I wouldn't have dared to throw it at any other man that fast – but he's got guts."

"Just the same," Joan said, "they'd better start rotating the station captains faster. The next man may not be so tough – and what if *he's* a sleepwalker?"

I didn't say anything. I'd had my share of worries for that week.

"You did a whale of a job yourself, Peter," Joan said. "I just wish we could bank it in the machine. We might need the data later."

"Well, why can't we?"

"The Joint Chiefs of Staff say no. They don't say why. But they don't want any part of it recorded in ULTIMAC – or anywhere else."

I stared at her. At first it didn't seem to make sense. And then it did – and that was worse.

"Wait a minute," I said. "Joan – does that mean what I think it means? Is 'Spatial Supremacy' just as bankrupt as 'Massive Retaliation' was? Is it possible that the satellite – and the bombs . . . Is it possible that I was telling Gascoigne the truth about the bombs being duds?"

Joan shrugged.

"He that darkeneth counsel without wisdom," she said, "isn't earning his salary."

Mistake Inside

This was England, two hundred years before bomb craters had become a fixed feature of the English landscape, and while the coffee house still had precedence over the pub. The fire roared, and the smoke from long clay church-warden pipes made a blue haze through which cheerful conversation struggled.

The door swung back, and the host stood in the opening, fat hands on hips, surveying the scene contentedly. Someone, invisible in the fog, drank a slurred uproarious toast, and a glass slammed into the fireplace, where the brandy-coated fragments made a myriad of small blue flames.

"Split me if that goes not in the reckoning!" the innkeeper bellowed. A ragged chorus of derision answered him. The inn cat shot down the stairs behind him, and its shadow glided briefly over the room as it passed the fire. It was an impossibly large, dark shadow, and for a moment it blacked out several of the booths in the rear of the chamber; the close, motionless air seemed to take on a chill. Then it was gone, and the cat, apparently annoyed by the noise, vanished into the depths of a heavy chair.

The host forgot about it. He was accustomed to its sedentary tastes. It often got sat on in the after-theater hilarity. He rolled good-naturedly across the room as someone pounded on a table for him.

But the cat, this time, had not merely burrowed into the cushions. It was gone. In the chair, in a curiously transparent

131

condition which made him nearly invisible in the uncertain light, sat a dazed, tired figure in a Twentieth-Century tux . . .

The radio was playing a melancholy opus called 'Is You Is or Is You Ain't, My Baby' as the cab turned the corner. "Here you are, sir," croaked the driver in his 3:00 A.M. voice.

The sleepy-eyed passenger's own voice was a little unreliable. "How much?"

The fare was paid and the cabby wearily watched his erstwhile customer go up the snow-covered walk between the hedges. He put the car in gear. Then he gaped and let the clutch up. The engine died with a reproachful gasp.

The late rider had staggered suddenly sidewise toward the bushes – had he been that drunk? Of course, he had only tripped and fallen out of sight; the cabby's fleeting notion that he had melted into the air was an illusion, brought on by the unchristian lateness of the hour. Nevertheless the tracks in the snow did stop rather unaccountably. The cabby swore, started his engine, and drove away, as cautiously as he had ever driven in his life.

Behind him, from the high trees in the yard, a cat released a lonely ululation on the cold, still night.

The stage was set . . .

There is order in all confusions; but Dr. Hugh Tracy, astronomer, knew nothing of the two events recorded above when his adventure began, so he could make no attempt at integrating them. Indeed, he was in confusion enough without dragging in any stray cats. One minute he had been charging at the door of Jeremy Wright's apartment, an automatic in his hand and blind rage in his heart. As his shoulder had splintered the panel, the world had revolved once around him, like a scene-changing stunt in the movies.

The scene had changed, all right. He was not standing in Jeremy Wright's apartment at all, but in a low-roofed,

132

dirt-floored room built of crudely shaped logs, furnished only with two antique chairs and a rickety table from which two startled men were arising. The two were dressed in leathern jerkins of a type fashionable in the early 1700's.

"I – I beg your pardon," he volunteered lamely. "I must have mixed the apartments up." He did not turn to go immediately, however, for as he thought disgustedly concerning the lengths to which some people will go to secure atmosphere, he noticed the dirty mullioned window across the room. The sight gave him a fresh turn. He might just possibly have mistaken the number of Jeremy Wright's apartment, but certainly he hadn't imagined running up several flights of stairs! Yet beyond the window he could see plainly a cheerful sunlit street.

Sunlit. The small fact that it had been 3:00 A.M. just a minute before did not help his state of mind.

"Might I ask what you're doing breaking out of my room in this fashion?" one of the queerly-costumed men demanded, glaring at Hugh. The other, a younger man, waved his hand indulgently at his friend and sat down again. "Relax, Jonathan," he said. "Can't you see he's a transportee?"

The older man stared more closely at the befuddled Dr. Tracy. "So it is," he said. "I swear, since Yero came to power again this country has been the dumping ground of half the universe. Wherever do they get such queer clothes, do you suppose?"

"Come on in," invited the other. "Tell us your story." He winked knowingly at Jonathan, and Hugh decided he did not like him.

"First," he said, "would you mind telling me something about the window?"

The two turned to follow his pointed finger. "Why, it's just an ordinary window, in that it shows what's beyond it," said the young man. "Why?"

"I wish I knew," Hugh groaned, closing his eyes and trying to remember a few childhood prayers. The only

133

one that came to mind was something about fourteen angels which hardly fitted the situation. After a moment he looked again, this time behind him. As he had suspected, the broken door did not lead back into the hallway of the apartment building, but into a small bedchamber of decidedly pre-Restoration cast.

"Take it easy," advised Jonathan. "It's hard to get used to at first. And put that thing away – it's a weapon of some kind, I suppose. The last transportee had one that spouted a streamer of purple gas. He was a very pleasant customer. What do you shoot?"

"Metal slugs," said Hugh, feeling faintly hysterical. "Where am I, anyhow?"

"Outside."

"Outside what?"

"That's the name of the country," the man explained patiently. "My name, by the way, is Jonathan Bell, and this gentleman is Oliver Martin."

"Hugh Tracy. Ph.D., F.R.A.S.," he added automatically. "So now I'm inside Outside, eh? How far am I from New York? I'm all mixed up."

"New York!" exclaimed Martin. "That's a new one. The last one said he was from Tir-nam-beo. At least I'd heard of that before. How did you get here, Tracy?"

"Suddenly," Tracy said succinctly. "One minute I was bashing at the door of Jeremy Wright's apartment, all set to shoot him and get my wife out of there; and then blooey!"

"Know this Wright fellow very well, or anything about him?"

"No, I've seen him once or twice, that's all. But I know Evelyn's been going to his place quite regularly while I was at the observatory."

Bell pulled a folded and badly soiled bit of paper from his breast pocket, smoothed it out on the splintery table top, and passed it to Hugh. "Look anything like this?" he asked.

"That's him! How'd you get this? Is he here somewhere?"

Bell and Martin both smiled. "It never fails," the younger man commented. "That's Yero, the ruler of this country during fall seasons. He just assumed power again three months ago. That picture comes off the town bulletin board, from a poster announcing his approaching marriage."

"Look," Hugh said desperately. "It isn't as if I didn't like your country, but I'd like to get back to my own. Isn't there some way I can manage it?"

"Sorry," Martin said. "We can't help you there. I suppose the best thing for you to do is to consult some licensed astrologer or thaumaturgist; he can tell you what to do. There are quite a few good magicians in this town – they all wind up here eventually – and one of them ought to be able to shoot you back where you belong."

"I don't put any stock in that humbug. I'm an astronomer."

"Not responsible for your superstitions. You asked for my advice, and I gave it."

"Astrologers!" Hugh groaned. "Oh, my lord!"

"However," Martin continued, "you can stay here with us for the time being. If you're an enemy of Yero, you're a friend of ours."

Hugh scratched his head. The mental picture of himself asking an astrologer for guidance did not please him.

"I suppose I'll have to make the best of this," he said finally. "Nothing like this ever happened to me before, or to anybody I've ever heard of, so I guess I'm more or less sane. Thanks for the lodging offer. Right now I'd like to go hunt up – ulp – a magician."

Bell smiled. "All right," he said, "if you get lost in the city, just ask around. They're friendly folk, and more of 'em than you think have been in your spot. Most of the shopkeepers know Bell's place. After you've wandered about a bit you'll get the layout better. Then we can discuss further plans."

Hugh wondered what kind of plans they were supposed

to discuss, but he was too anxious to discover the nature of the place into which he had fallen to discuss the question further. Bell led him down a rather smelly hallway to another door, and in a moment he found himself surveying the street.

It was all incredibly confusing. The language the two had spoken was certainly modern English, yet the busy, narrow thoroughfare was just as certainly Elizabethan in design. The houses all had overhanging second stories. Through the very center of the cobbled street ran a shallow gutter in which a thin stream of swill-like liquid trickled. The bright light flooding the scene left no doubt as to its reality, and yet there was still the faint aura of question about it. The feeling was intensified when he discovered that there was no sun; the whole dome of sky was an even dazzle. It was all like a movie set, and it was a surprise to find that the houses had backs to them.

Across the street, perched comfortably in the cool shadows of a doorway, an old man slept, a tasselled nightcap hanging down over his forehead. Over his head a sign swayed: COPPERSMITH. Not ten feet away from him a sallow young man was leaning against the wall absorbed in the contents of a very modern-looking newspaper, which bore the headlines: DOWSER CONFESSES FAIRY GOLD PLANT. Lower down on the page Hugh could make out a boxed item: STILETTO KILLER FEIGNS INSANITY. In a moment, he was sure, he wouldn't have to feign it. The paper was as jarring an anachronism in the Shakespearean street scene as a six-cylinder coupe would have been.

At least he was spared having to account for any cars, though. The conventional mode of transportation was horses, it seemed. Every so often one would canter past recklessly. Their riders paid little regard to the people under their horses' hoofs and the people in their turn scattered with good-natured oaths, like any group of twentieth century pedestrians before a taxi.

As Hugh stepped off the low stone lintel he heard a

breathy whistle, and turning, beheld a small red-headed urchin coming jerkily toward him. The boy was alternately whistling and calling "Here, Fleet, Fleet, Fleet! Nice doggy! Here, Fleet!" His mode of locomotion was very peculiar; he lunged mechanically from side to side or forward as if he were a machine partly out of control.

As he came closer Hugh saw that he was holding a forked stick in his hands, the foot of the Y pointing straight ahead, preceding the lad no matter where he went. On the boy's head was a conical blue cap lettered with astrological and alchemical symbols, which had sagged so as to completely cover one eye, but he seemed loath to let go of the stick to adjust it.

In a moment the boy had staggered to a stop directly before Hugh, while the rigid and quivering end of the stick went down to Hugh's shoes and began slowly to ascend. He was conscious of a regular sniffing sound.

"Better tend to that cold, son," he suggested.

"That isn't me, it's the rod," the boy said desperately. "Please, sir, have you seen a brown puppy — " At this point the stick finished its olfactory inspection of Hugh and jerked sidewise, yanking the boy after it. As the urchin disappeared still calling "Here, Fleet!" Hugh felt a faint shiver. Here was the first evidence of a working magic before his eyes, and his sober astronomer's soul recoiled from it.

A window squealed open over his head, and he jumped just in time to avoid a gush of garbage which was flung casually down toward the gutter. Thereafter he clung as close to the wall as he could, and kept beneath the overhanging second stories. Walking thus, with his eyes on the sole-punishing cobbles, deep in puzzlement, his progress was presently arrested by collision with a mountain.

When his eyes finally reached the top of it, it turned out to be a man, a great muscular thug clad in expensive blue velvet small-clothes and a scarlet cape like an eighteenth century exquisite. Was there no stopping this kaleidoscope of anachronism?

137

"Weah's ya mannas?" the apparition roared. "Move out!"

"What for?" Hugh replied in his austere classroom tone. "I don't care to be used as a sewage pail any more than you do."

"Ah," said the giant. "Wise guy, eh? Dunno ya bettas, eh?" There was a whistling sound as he drew a thin sword which might have served to dispatch whales. Hugh's Royal Society reserve evaporated and he clawed frantically for his automatic, but before the double murder was committed the giant lowered his weapon and bent to stare more closely at the diminutive doctor.

"Ah," he repeated. "Ya a transportee, eh?"

"I guess so," Tracy said, remembering that Martin had used the word.

"Weah ya from?"

"Brooklyn," Hugh said hopefully.

The giant shook his head. "Weah you guys think up these here names is a wonda. Well, ya dunno the customs, that's easy t'see."

He stepped aside to let Hugh pass.

"Thank you," said Hugh with a relieved sigh. "Can you tell me where I can find an astrologer?" He still could not pronounce the word without choking.

"Ummmm – most of 'em are around the squaah. Ony, juss between you an' me, buddy, I'd keep away from there till the p'rade's ova. Yero's got an orda out fa arrestin' transportees." The giant nodded pleasantly. "Watch ya step." He stalked on down the street.

Looking after him, Hugh was startled to catch a brief glimpse of a man dressed in complete dinner clothes, including top hat, crossing the street and rounding a corner. Hoping that this vision from his own age might know something significant about this screwy world, he ran after him, but lost him in the traffic. He found nothing but a nondescript and unhappy alleycat which ran at his approach.

* * *

138

Discouraged, Hugh went back the way he had come and set out in search of the public square and an astrologer. As he walked, he gradually became conscious of a growing current of people moving in the same direction, a current which was swelled by additions from every street and byway they passed. There was a predominance of holiday finery, and he remembered the giant's words about a parade. Well, he'd just follow the crowd; it would make finding the square that much easier.

Curious snatches of conversation reached his ears as he plodded along. "... Aye, in the square, sir; one may hope that it bodes us some change ..." "... Of Yero eke, that a younge wyfe he gat his youthe agoon, and withal ..." "... An' pritnear every time dis guy toins up, yiz kin count on gittin' it in the neck ..." "... Oft Seyld Yero sceathena threatum, hu tha aethlingas ellen fremedon ..."

Most of the fragments were in English, but English entirely and indiscriminantly mixed as to century. Hugh wondered if the few that sounded foreign were actually so, or whether they were some Saxon or Jutish ancestor of English – or, perhaps, English as it might sound in some remote future century. If that latter were so, then there might be other cities in Outside where only old, modern and future French was spoken, or Russian, or —

The concept was too complex to entertain. He remembered the giant's warning, and shook his head. This world, despite the obvious sweating reality of the crowd around him and the lumpy pavement beneath his feet, was still too crazy to be anything but a phantom. He was curious to see this Yero, who looked so inexplicably like Jeremy Wright, but he could not take any warning of Outside very seriously. His principal concern was to get back inside again.

As the part of the crowd which bore him along debouched from the narrow street into a vast open space, he heard in the distance the sound of trumpets, blowing a complicated fanfare. A great shouting went up, but somehow it seemed not the usual cheering of expectant parade-goers. There was a strange undertone – perhaps of animosity? Hugh could not tell.

In the press he found that he could move neither forward nor back. He would have to stand where he was until the event was over and the mob dispersed.

By craning his neck over the shoulders of those in front of him – a procedure which, because of his small stature, involved some rather precarious teetering on tip-toe – he could see across the square. It was surrounded on all four sides by houses and shops, but the street which opened upon it directly opposite him was a wide one. Through it he saw a feature of the city which the close-grouped overhanging houses had hidden before – a feature which put the finishing touch upon the sense of unreality and brought back once more the suggestion of a vast set for a Merrie-England movie by a bad director.

It was a castle. Furthermore it was twice as big as any real castle ever was, and its architecture was totally out of the period of the town below it. It was out of any period. It was a modernist's dream, a Walter Gropius design come alive. The rectangular facade and flanking square pylons were vaguely reminiscent of an Egyptian temple of Amenhotep IV's time, but the whole was of bluely gleaming metal, shimmering smoothly in the even glare of the sky.

From the flat summits floated scarlet banners bearing an unreadable device. A clustered group of these pennons before the castle seemed to be moving, and by stretching his neck almost to the snapping point Hugh could see that they were being carried by horsemen who were coming slowly down the road. Ahead of them came the trumpeters, who were now entering the square, sounding their atonal tocsin.

Now the trumpeters passed abreast of him, and the crowd made a lane to let them through. Next came the bearers of the standards, two by two, holding their horses' heads high. A group of richly dressed but ruffianly retainers followed

140

them. The whole affair reminded Hugh of a racketeer's funeral in Chicago's prohibition days. Finally came the sedan chair which bore the royal couple – and Dr. Hugh Tracy at last lost hold of his sanity. For beside the aloof, hated Yero-Jeremy in the palanquin was Evelyn Tracy.

When Hugh came back to his senses he was shouting unintelligible epithets, and several husky townsmen were holding his arms. "Easy, Bud," one of them hissed into his ear. "Haven't you ever seen him before?"

Hugh forced himself back to a semblance of calmness, and had sense enough to say nothing of Evelyn. "Who – what is he?" he gasped. The other looked at him tensely for a moment, then, reassured, let go of him.

"That's Yero. He's called many names, but the most common is The Enemy. Better get used to seeing him. You can't help hating him, but it'll do you no good to fly off the handle like that."

"You mean everybody hates him?"

The townsman frowned. "Why certainly. He's The Enemy."

"Then why don't you throw him out?"

"Well — "

The other burgher, who had said nothing thus far, broke in: "Presenuk prajolik solda, soldama mera per ladsua hrutkai; per stanisch felemetskje droschnovar."

"Exactly," said the other man. "You okay now, Bud?"

"Ulp," Hugh said. "Yes, I'm all right."

The crowd, still roaring its ambiguous cheer, was following the procession out the other end of the square, and shortly Hugh found himself standing almost alone. A sign over a nearby shop caught his eye: *Dr. ffoni, Licensed Magician.* Here was what he had been looking for. As he ran quickly across the square toward the rickety building he thought he caught a glimpse out of the tail of his eyes of a top hat moving along in the departing crowd, but he dismissed it. That could wait.

The shop was dark inside, and at first he thought it empty. But in answer to repeated shouts a scrambling began in the back room, and a nondescript little man entered, struggling into a long dark gown several sizes too large for him.

"Sorry," he puffed, trying to regain his right hand, which he had lost down the wrong sleeve, "out watching the parade. May I serve you, young sir?"

"Yes. I'm a transportee, and I'd like to get back where I belong."

"So would we all, so would we all, indeed," said the magician, nodding vigorously. "Junior!"

"Yes, paw." A gawky adolescent peered out of the back room.

"Customer."

"Ah, paw. I don' wanna go in t' any trance. I'm dragging a rag-bag to a rat-race t'night an' I wanna be groovy. You know prognostics allus knock me flatter'n a mashed-potato san'witch."

"You'll do as you're told, or I'll not allow you to use the broomstick. You see, young sir," the magician addressed Hugh, "familiar spirits are at somewhat of a premium around here, there being so many in this town in my profession; but since my wife was a Sybil, my son serves me adequately in commissions of this nature."

He turned back to the boy, who was now sitting on a stool behind the counter, and produced a pink lollipop from the folds of his robe. The boy allowed it to be placed in his mouth docilely enough, and closed his eyes. Hugh watched, not knowing whether to laugh or to swear. If this idiotic procedure produced results, he was sure he'd never be able to contemplate Planck's Constant seriously again.

"Now then, while we're waiting," the sorcerer continued, "you should understand the situation. All living has two sides, the IN-side and the OUT-side. The OUT-side is where the roots of significant mistakes are embedded; the IN-side where they flower. Since most men have their backs turned to the OUT-side all their lives, few mistakes can be rectified. But if a man turns, as if on a pivot, so that he faces the other way, he may see and be on the OUT-side, and have the opportunity to uproot his error if he can find the means. Such a fortunate man is a transportee."

"So, in effect, existence has just been given a half-turn around me, to put me facing outside instead of inside where I belong?"

"A somewhat egotistical way of putting it, but that is the general idea. The magicians of many ages have used this method of disposing of their enemies; for unless the transportee can find his Avatars – the symbols, as it were, of his error – and return them to their proper places, he must remain Outside forever. This last many have done by choice, since none ever dies Outside."

"I'd just as soon not," Hugh said with a groan. "What are my Avatars?"

"To turn a capstan there must be a lever, and to pivot a man Outside means that two other living beings must act as the ends of this lever, and exchange places in time, while you stood still in time and space, but were pivoted to face Outside."

At this point he reached over to the boy and gave an experimental tug on the protruding stick of the lollipop. It slipped out easily; all the pink candy had dissolved. "Ah," he said. "We are about ready." He made a few passes with his hands and began to sing:

> "*Jet propulsion, Dirac hole,*
> *Trochilminthes, Musterole,*
> *Plenum, bolide, Ding an sich,*
> *Shoot the savvy to me, Great White Which!*"

The tune was one more commonly associated with Pepsi-Cola. After a moment the boy's mouth opened, and licking the remains of the lollipop from its corners, he said clearly, "Two hundred. Night prowlers."

"Is that all?" Hugh said, not much surprised.

"That's quite enough. Well, maybe not quite enough, but it's about all I ever get."

"But what does it mean?"

"Why, simply this: that your Avatars are two hundred years apart from each other; and that they are night-prowlers."

"Two hundred years! and I have to find them?"

"They are represented by simulacra in Outside. You must identify these simulacra and touch each one; this done, they will exchange again, and you will be rotated Inside. Have you seen any here?"

A light burst in Hugh's brain. "I saw a man from my own age who looked like a bona-fide night-prowler all right."

"You see?" The magician spread his hands expressively. "Half the work is over. Simply search for another might-prowler whose costume is two hundred years older – or, of course, younger – than the first. It's very simple. Now, young sir — " The hands began to wash each other suggestively.

Hugh produced a handful of coins. "That's no good," said the little man with a sniff. "I can make that myself. It's the city's principal industry. I don't suppose you have any sugar on you? Or rubber bands? No? Hmm. How about that?"

He prodded Hugh's vest. "That" was Hugh's Sigma Chi key, dangling from his watch chain. He had been elected to the honorary society by virtue of a closely reasoned paper on the deficiencies of current stellar evolution hypotheses. With a grin he passed it across the counter. "Thanks," the thaumaturgist said, "I collect fetishes. Totem fixation, I guess."

Feeling rather humble, Hugh left the shop and started back toward Bell's house by the most direct route his memory could provide. Now that he had begun to get his bearings, his stomach was reminding him that he had gone the whole day without food. On the way he saw the known Avatar half-way down a dark alley, contemplating a low doorway sorrowfully; but when he arrived, the top-hatted figure was gone. By the time he entered the house where he had had his first glimpse of Outside, he was decidedly discouraged, but the pleasant smell of food revived him somewhat.

"Good evening," Bell greeted him, though the ambiguous daylight was as unvaryingly bright as ever. "Find your astrologer?"

"Yes. Now I have to find a night-prowler. You wouldn't be one, by any chance?"

The man laughed softly. "In a sense, yes, but I'm too old to be the one you want. You're Avatar-hunting, I take it?"

"That's it."

"Well, I'm not a simulacrum. I'm a native here, one of the original settlers. Come on and eat, anyhow." He led the way into the room which Hugh had first seen, and waved him to the table. On it was a platter bearing a complete roast hog's head with an apple in its mouth and three strips of bacon between its ears, a pudding, a meat pie, a spitted duckling, three wooden trenchers – boards used as plates – and three razor-sharp knives. Obviously forks were not in style Outside.

"Has Yero's administration caused a potato shortage?" Hugh asked curiously.

"Potato? No. You transportees have odd ideas; you mean potatoes to eat? Don't you know they're a relative of the deadly nightshade?"

Hugh shrugged and fell to. There was bread anyhow. During the course of the meal the two pumped him about his experiences during the day, and he answered with increasing caution. They seemed to be up to something. He especially disliked young Martin, whose knowing smile when Hugh described his belief that Yero's queen was in actuality his own wife irritated him. As the dinner ended Bell came to the point.

"You've heard Yero spoken of as The Enemy? Well, his rule here is intermittent. He just pops up every fall season and takes the place of the Old One, who is the only rightful

145

king, and a good one. It's during Yero's ascendancy that all the transportees show up – all the people who make mistakes during that period, if the mistakes are of a certain kind, get pivoted around here to correct them. It gets pretty nuisancy.

"You can see what I mean. Here you come busting in on us and split our good pine door and eat one third of our food. Not that we begrudge you the food; you're welcome to it; but it is a bother to have all these strangers around. In addition it decreases the future population in a way I haven't time to describe now. Everybody hates Yero, even the transportees. It's our idea to assassinate him before he gets to come back another time; then the Old One can really do us some good and the town can come back to normal. Sounds reasonable, doesn't it?"

"I thought no one ever died here."

"Nobody ever does, naturally, but accidents or violence can distribute an individual to the point of helplessness. Since you seem to hate Yero like the rest of us, we thought you might like to throw in with us."

The hospitality of the two did not permit him to refuse immediately, but more and more he was sure he did not want to be involved in any project of theirs. Bell's picture of what Outside's substitute for death was like revolted him; and in addition, the thought occurred to him that it would be dangerous to take any positive steps while he was still ignorant of the error that had brought him here.

"I'd like to sleep on that," he said cautiously. "Do you mind if I defer judgment for the night? I haven't had any sleep for thirty-six hours, and I'll just pass out, if I don't get some."

"All right," Bell said. "You think it over. With The Enemy out of the way it might be easier to find your Avatars, too, you know. Nothing ever works right while he's in power."

When Hugh awoke his brain did not function properly for quite a few seconds. The bed had had fleas in it, and

146

the changeless brilliancy of the 'daylight' had kept him awake a long time despite his exhaustion. The sight of the black-clad figure seated on the nearby stool did not register at first.

"Good mornin'," he said muzzily. Then, "You!"

"Me," the man in the top hat replied ungrammatically. "I had to wait for the two Princes to get out of the house before I could see you. I've been looking for you."

"*You've* been looking for *me*," Hugh repeated angrily, sitting up in bed. He noticed with only faint surprise that the wall of the room was plainly visible through the visitant's shirt bosom. "Well, you'll have to solidify a minute if you're going to do me any good. I'm supposed to touch you."

"Not yet. When you do, this image will vanish, and I've got a few things to talk to you about before that happens. I got bounced back two hundred years in time past on account of a fool mistake you made, and I'm as anxious to see you straightened out as you are yourself." He hiccuped convulsively. "Luckily I'm a book collector with a special bent towards Cruikshank. I had sense enough to consult Dr. Lee while I was behind the times, and found out where you were. Do you know?"

"Where am I? Why, I'm Outside."

"Use your noggin. How much does 'Outside' mean to you, anyhow?"

"Very little," Hugh agreed. "Well, the only other place I know where people go that make mistakes is – awk! Now, wait a minute! Don't tell me — "

The figure nodded solemnly. "Now you've got it. You should have guessed that when the Princes told you their boss was called the Old One. You've already had clue after clue that they're forbidden to conceal from you; that no one dies here; that all the world's magicians come here eventually; that making money – remember the saying about the root of all evil? – is the town's principal industry; and so on."

147

"Well, well." Hugh scratched his head. "Hugh Tracy, Ph.D., FRAS, spending a season in Hell just like Rimbaud or some other crazy poet. The fall season at that. How Evelyn would love this. But it's not quite as I would have pictured it."

"Why should it have been?"

Hugh could think of no answer. "Who's Yero, then? He's called The Enemy."

"He's their enemy, sure enough. I don't know exactly who he is, but he's someone in authority, and his job is to see the Purgatory candidates get a chance to straighten things out for themselves. Naturally the Fallen buck him as much as possible; and part of the trick is to disguise the place somewhat, to keep its nature hidden from the transportees – the potential damned – and lure them into doing something that will keep them here for good. That bed you're in, for instance, is probably a pool of flaming brimstone or something of the sort."

Hugh bounded out hastily.

"Yero establishes himself in the fortress of Dis, which is what that pile of chromium junk is, up on the hill, after you get behind the disguise. Each time he comes, he makes a tour through the town, showing himself to each newcomer in a form which will mean the most to that person. The important thing is that few people take kindly to being corrected in the fundamental kinds of mistakes that bring them here, so that nine times out of ten Yero's appearance to you makes you hate him."

"Hmm," Hugh said. "I begin to catch on, around the edges, as it were. To me he looked like a man I'd started out to murder a few days ago."

"You're on the track. Examine your motives, use your head, son, and don't let the Princes trick you into anything." The pellucid shape steadied and grew real and solid by degrees; the man in the top hat rose and walked toward the bed. "Above all – don't hate Yero."

148

His outstretched hand touched Hugh's sleeve, and he vanished on the instant with a sharp hiccup.

There was no one in the house, and nothing to eat but a half-consumed and repellent-looking pudding left over from the 'night' before, which he finished for lack of anything else rather than out of any attraction the suety object had as a breakfast dish. Then he left the house in search of the other Avatar.

The light was bright and cheerful as always, but he felt chilly all the same. Discovering where he was had destroyed all of his amusement in the town's crazy construction, and taken the warmth out of his bones. He eyed the passers-by uneasily, wondering as each one approached him whether he was seeing someone like himself, a soul in eternal torment, or an emissary of the Fallen whose real form was ambiguous.

For the rest of the morning he roamed the streets in search of a likely-looking figure, but finally he had to admit that his wanderings were fruitless. He sat down on a doorstep to think it out.

His Avatars were the 'symbols of his error'; they were night-prowlers, obviously, because he had been one himself, gun in hand. The error itself was something to do with Jeremy Wright and Evelyn – not the impending murder, because it had not been committed, but some other error. The man in the top hat had been chosen, perhaps, because he had conceived of Wright as a cavalier, a suave home-breaker, or something of the sort; dinner clothes made a pointed symbol of such a notion. Of what else, specifically, had he suspected Jeremy? Tom-catting!

He groaned and dropped his head in his hands, remembering the cat he had seen in conjunction with his first sight of the man in dinner clothes. How was he to find one ragged alley-cat in a town where there were doubtless hundreds? Cats did not wear period costumes. He couldn't go around touching cats until something happened!

He heard a sniffing sound and a thin mournful whine at his side. He looked down.

"Go 'way," he said. "I want a cat, not a mongrel pooch."

The puppy, recoiling at the unfriendly tone, dropped its tail and began to sidle away from him, and gloomily he watched it go. Brown dog? – Brown cat? – Brown dog! An inspiration!

"Here, Fleet," he essayed. The puppy burst into a frenzy of tail-wagging and came back, with that peculiar angled trot only dogs out of all the four-footed beasts seem to affect. Hugh patted its head, and it whined and licked his hand.

"There, there," he said. "You're lost, I know. So am I. If your name is Fleet, we'll both be home shortly. It darn well better be Fleet."

Hugh considered the animal speculatively. It certainly seemed to respond to the name; but then, it was only a puppy, and might just as easily respond to any friendly noise. Grimly he sat and waited. In about an hour the dog began to get restless, and Hugh carted it across the street to a shop and bought it some meat, leaving in payment a letter from a colleague which the shopkeeper seemed to think was full of cantrips, charms of some kind. Then he resumed his vigil.

It was approximately four o'clock by his personal time-keeping system when he finally heard the sound he had been listening for, but not daring to expect – the voice of the red-headed urchin, calling his dog's name in incredibly weary tones. In a moment the boy appeared, his face tear-streaked, his feet stumbling, his eyes heavy from lack of sleep. The stick was still pulling him, and the conical cap, by a miracle, still rested askew on his head. The rod lunged forward eagerly as soon as it pointed toward Hugh, and the boy stopped by the doorstep, the divining rod pointing in quivering triumph squarely at the puppy. The boy sat down in the street and began to bawl.

"Now, now," said Hugh. "You've found your dog. Don't cry. What's the matter?"

"I haven't had any sleep or any food," the boy snuffled. "I couldn't let go, and the dog could move faster than I could, so I've been pulled all over the city, and I'll bet it's all the Old One's fault, too — " His voice rose rapidly and Hugh tried to calm him down, a little abstractedly, for in the reference to the Old One, Hugh had recognised the boy's real nature, and knew him for an ally. Wait till I tell Evelyn, he told himself, that I've seen an Archangel and one of the Cherubim face to face, and hatched plots with the Fallen!

"I saw your dog, and figured probably you'd be along."

"Oh, thank you, sir. I guess I'd have spent the rest of eternity chasing him if you hadn't held him until I could catch up with him." He looked angrily at the forked stick, which now lay inert and innocuous on the cobbled pavement. "I used the wrong spell, and it had to smell people. No wonder we could never get close enough to Fleet for him to hear me!"

"Do you think you could make the rod work again?"

"Oh, yes, sir. Only I never would."

"I want to use it. Do you mind?"

"I don't mind. It's my uncle's, but I can always cut another one. Only it won't work without the hat, and I took that from my uncle too. He's an Authority," the urchin added proudly. Hugh thought of Goethe's Sorcerer's Apprentice and grinned.

"How come you didn't shake your head and knock it off when you got tired?"

"Oh, the hat only starts it. After that it goes by itself. I just didn't want to lose my uncle's hat, that's all."

"Good for you. Then suppose I borrow the hat for just a minute, and you grab it when the stick starts. I want to find a cat."

The boy shook his head doubtfully. "I wouldn't want to do it myself, but it's your business. What kind of cat? I have to make up a spell."

151

Hugh anticipated some difficulty in explaining what it was he wanted, but to his relief the boy had already recognised him as a transportee and understood at once.

"All right. Put the hat on. Pick up the stick like I had it. That's it, one fork in each hand. Now then:

> *"Seeker of souls, lost boys and girls,*
> *Of objects and of wells,*
> *Find his gate between the worlds*
> *Before the curfew knells;*
> *Find the cat who should reside*
> *In the mortal world Inside."*

The divining rod started forward with a terrific jerk, and Hugh plunged after it. The boy ran alongside him and snatched off the magician's cap. "Thanks," Hugh shouted. "You're welcome," the boy called after him. "Good luck, sir, and thank you for holding my dog." Then the stick hauled Hugh around a corner, and the dog-owner was gone; but in Hugh's mind there remained a split-second glimpse of a strange smile, mischievous, kindly, and agelessly wise.

The cherub had not specified in his incantation which sense the rod was to use, and so it had chosen the quickest one – intuition, or supersensory-perception, or sixth-sense – Hugh had heard it called many things, but until he held the ends of the fork he had never quite comprehended what it was.

The stick drew him faster. His toes seemed barely to touch the hard cobbles. Almost it seemed as if he were about to fly. Yet, somehow, there was no wind in his face, nor any real sensation of speed. All about him was a breathless quiet, an intent hush of light through which he soared. The houses and shops of the town sped by him, blurred and sadly unreal. The outlines danced waveringly in a haze of heat.

The town was changing.

Fear lodged a prickly lump in his larynx. The facades

were going down as he came closer to his own world. He knew that before long the conventional disguises of the town would be melted, and Hell would begin to show through. Startled faces turned to watch him as he passed, and their features were not as they should be. Once he was sure he had confronted Bell and Martin for an instant.

A cry, distant and wild, went up behind him. It had been Bell – or was it – Belial? Other feet were running beside his own; shortly there were other cries, and then a gathering roar and tumult of voices; the street began to throb dully with the stampeding feet of a great mob. The rod yanked him down an alleyway. The thunder followed.

In the unreal spaces of the public square the other entrances were already black with blurred figures howling down upon him. The stick did not falter, but rushed headlong toward the castle. His hands sweated profusely on the fork, and his feet skimmed the earth in great impossible bounds. The gates of the fortress swept toward him. There were shadowy guards there, but they were looking through him at the mob behind; the next instant he was passing them.

The mists of unreality became thick, translucent. Everything around him was a vague reddish opalescence through which the sounds of the herd rioted, seemingly from every direction. Suddenly he was sure he was surrounded; but the rod arrowed forward regardless, and he had to follow.

At last the light began to coalesce, and in a moment he saw floating before him a shining crystal globe, over which floated the illuminated faces of his wife – and – Yero, The Enemy. This was the crucial instant, and he remembered the simulacrum's advice: "Don't hate Yero."

Indeed, he could not. He had nearly forgotten whom it was that Yero resembled, so great was his desire for escape, and his fear of the tumult behind him.

The light grew, and by it, the table upon which the crystal rested, and the bodies belonging to the two illuminated heads, became slowly visible. There was a cat there, too; he saw the outline become sharp as he catapulted on through the dimness. He tried to slow down as he approached the table. The rod, this time, did not resist. The two heads regarded him with slow surprise. The cat began to rise and bristle.

The shouting died.

"Hugh!"

He was in Jeremy Wright's apartment, a splintered door behind him, his heels digging into the carpet to halt his headlong charge. In his outstretched hand was, not a warped divining rod, but a gun.

"Hugh!" his wife cried again. "You found out! But — "

The table was still there, and the crystal. The cat and the castle were gone. But Jeremy Wright was still dressed in the robes of an astrologer. He *was* an astrologer.

"I'm sorry, darling, honestly – I knew you hated it, but – after all, breaking in this way! And – a gun! After all, even if you *do* think it's humbug — "

Hugh looked at the serene face of Jeremy Wright, and silently pocketed the automatic. There was nothing, after all, that he could have said to either of them.

A Dusk of Idols

I can tell you now what happened to Naysmith. He hit Chandala.

Quite by coincidence – he was on his way home at the time – but it caught him. It was in all respects a most peculiar accident. The chances were against it, including that I should have heard anything about it.

Almost everyone in Arm II knows that Chandala is, pre-eminently among civilized planets, a world in mortal agony – and a world about which, essentially, nothing can be done. Naysmith didn't know it. He had had no experience of Arm II and was returning along it from his first contact with the Heart stars when his ship (and mine) touched Chandala briefly. He was on his way back to Earth (which technically is an Arm II planet, but so far out in the hinterlands that no Earthman ever thinks of it as such) when this happened, and since it happened during ship's night, he would never have known the difference if it hadn't been for an attack of simple indigestion which awakened him – and me.

It's very hard to explain the loss of so eminent a surgeon as Naysmith without maligning his character, but as his only confidant, more or less, I don't seem to have much of a choice. The fact is that he should have been the last person in the Galaxy to care about Chandala's agony. He had used his gifts to become exclusively a rich man's surgeon; as far as I know, he had never done any time in a clinic after his residency days. He had gone to the Heart stars only to sterilize, for a very large fortune in fees, the sibling of the Bbiben of Bbenaf – for the fees, and for the additional fortune the honor would bring him later. Bbenaf law requires that the operation be performed by an off-worlder, but Naysmith was the first Earthman to be invited to do it.

But if during the trip there or back some fellow passenger had come down with a simple appendicitis, Naysmith wouldn't have touched him. He would have said, with remote impartiality, that that was the job of the ship's surgeon (me). If for some reason I had been too late to help, Naysmith still would not have lifted a finger.

There are not supposed to be any doctors like that, but there are. Nobody should assume that I think they are in the majority – they are in fact very rare – but I see no point in pretending that they don't exist. They do; and the eminent Naysmith was one of them. He was in fact almost the Platonic ideal of such a doctor. And you do not have to be in the Heart stars to begin to think of the Hippocratic Oath as being quaint, ancient, and remote. You can become isolated from it just as easily on Earth, by the interposition of unclimbable mountains of money, if you share Naysmith's temperament.

His temperament, to put it very simply, was that of a pathologically depressed man carrying a terrible load of anxiety. In him, it showed up by making him a hypochondriac, and I don't think he would ever have gone into medicine at all had it not been for an urgent concern about his own health which set in while he was still in college. I had known him slightly then, and was repelled by him. He was always thinking about his own innards. Nothing pleased him, nothing took him out of himself, he had no eye for any of the elegance and the beauty of the universe outside his own skin. Though he was as brilliant a man as I ever knew, he was a bore, the kind of bore who replies to "How are you?" by telling you how he is, in clinical detail. He was forever certain that

156

his liver or his stomach or some other major organ had just quit on him and was going to have to be removed – probably too suddenly for help to be summoned in time.

It seems inarguable to me, though I am not a psychologist, that he took up medicine primarily in the hope (unrecognized in his own mind) of being able to assess his own troubles better, and treat them himself when he couldn't get another doctor to take them as seriously as he did. Of course this did not work. It is an old proverb in medicine that the man who treats himself has a fool for a physician, which is only a crude way of saying that the doctor-patient relationship absolutely requires that there be two people involved. A man can no more be his own doctor than he can be his own wife, no matter how much he knows about marriage or medicine.

The result was that even after becoming the kind of surgeon who gets called across 50,000 light-years to operate on the sibling of the Bbiben of Bbenaf, he was still a hypochondriac. In fact, he was worse off than ever, because he now had the most elaborate and sophisticated knowledge of all the obscure things that might be wrong with him. He had a lifelong case of intern's syndrome, the cast of mind which makes beginners in medicine sure that they are suffering from everything they have just read about in the textbook. He knew this; he was, as I have said, a brilliant man; though he had reached his ostensible goal, he was now in a position where he did not *dare* to treat himself, even for the hiccups.

And this was why he called me at midnight, ship's time, to look him over. There was nothing curable the matter with him. He had eaten something on Bbenaf – though he was a big, burly, bearded man, immoderate eating had made him unpleasantly soft – that was having trouble accommodating itself to his Terrestrial protein complement. I judged that tomorrow he would have a slight rash, and thereafter the episode would be over. I told him so.

"Um. Yes. Daresay you're right. Still rather a shock

157

though, to be brought bolt upright like that in the middle of the night."

"Of course. However I'm sure it's nothing more than a slight food allergy – the commonest of all tourist complaints," I added, a little maliciously. "The tablets are antihistaminic, of course. They ought to head off any serious sequelae, and make you a little sleepy to boot. You could use the relaxation, I think."

He nodded absently, without taking any apparent notice of my mean little dig. He did not recognize me, I was quite sure. It had been a long time since college.

"Where are we?" he said. He was wide awake, though his alarm reaction seemed to be wearing off, and he didn't seem to want to take my hint that he use the pills as sleepy drugs; he wanted company, at least for a little while. Well, I was curious, too. He was an eminent man in my own profession, and I had an advantage over him: I knew more about him than he thought I did. If he wanted to talk, I was delighted to let him.

"Chandala, I believe. A real running sore of a planet, but we won't be here long; it's just a message stop."

"Oh? What's the matter with the place? Barbaric?"

"No, not in the usual sense. It's classified as a civilized planet. It's just sick, that's all. Most of the population is being killed off."

"A pandemic?" Naysmith said slowly. "That doesn't sound like a civilized planet."

"It's hard to explain," I said. "It's not just one plague. There are scores of them going. I suppose the simple way to put it is to say that the culture of Chandala doesn't believe in sanitation – but that's not really true either. They believe in it, thoroughly, but they don't practice it very much. In fact a large part of the time they practice it in reverse."

"In reverse? That doesn't make any sense."

"I warned you it was hard to explain. I mean that public health there is a privilege. The ruling classes make

158

it unavailable to the people they govern, as a means of keeping them in line."

"But that's insane!" Naysmith exclaimed.

"I suppose it is, by our ideas. It's obviously very hard to keep under control, anyhow; the rulers often suffer as much as the ruled. But all governments are based on the monopoly of the right to use violence – only the weapons vary from planet to planet. This one is Chandala's. And the Heart stars have decided not to interfere."

He fell silent. I probably had not needed to remind him that what the federation we call the Heart stars decided to do, or not to do, was often very difficult to riddle. Its records reach back about a million years, which however cover only its period of stability. Probably it is as much as twice that old. No Arm II planet belonged to the group yet. Earth could be expected to be allowed to join in about forty-five thousand years – and that was what remained of half our originally allotted trial period; the cut was awarded us after our treaty with the star-dwelling race of Angels. In the meantime, we could expect no help . . . nor could Chandala. Earth was fortunate to be allowed any intercourse whatsoever with the Heart stars; there again, we could thank the Angels – who live forever – for vouching for us.

"Dr. Rosenbaum," Naysmith said slowly, "do you think that's right and proper?"

So he had recognized me after all. He would never have bothered to look up my name on the roster.

"Well, no, I suppose not. But the rule is that every planet is to be allowed to go to hell in its own handbasket. It isn't my rule, or the Earth's rule; but there it is. The Heart stars just won't be bothered with any world that can't achieve stability by itself. They have seen too many of them come and go."

"I think there's more to it than that. Some of the planets that failed to get into the federation failed because they got into planetwide wars – or into wars with each other."

"Sure," I said, puzzled. "That's just the kind of thing the Heart stars have no use for."

"So they didn't interfere to stop the wars."

"No." Now I was beginning to see what he was driving at, but he bore down on me relentlessly all the same.

"So there is in fact no Heart-star rule that we can't help Chandala if we want to. In fact, doing so may not even prejudice our case with the federation. We just don't know."

"I suppose that's true, but — "

"And, in fact, it might help us? We don't know that either?"

"No, we don't," I admitted, but my patience was beginning to run out. It had been a long night. "All we do know is that the Heart stars follow certain rules of their own. Common sense suggests that our chances would be best if we followed them, too."

"Common sense for our remotely imaginable great-great-greatest of grandchildren, maybe. But by then conditions will have changed beyond our remotest imaginings. Half a millennium!"

"They don't change in the Heart stars. That's the whole point–stability. And above all, I'd avoid picking up a stick of TDX like Chandala. It's obviously just the kind of non-survival planet the Heart stars *mean* to exclude by their rules. There'd be nothing you could do with it but blow yourself up. And there's obviously nothing we could do *for* it, anyhow!"

"Gently now, Doctor. Are you sure of that? Sanitation isn't the only public-health technique there is."

"I don't follow you," I said. The fact is that by now I wasn't trying very hard.

"Well," Naysmith said, "consider that there was once a thing called the Roman Empire. It owned all the known world and lasted many centuries. But fifty men with modern weapons could have conquered it, even when it was at its most powerful."

"But the Heart stars — "

"I am not talking about the Heart stars. I'm talking about Chandala. Two physicians with modern field kits could have wiped out almost all the diseases that raddled the Roman Empire. For instance, you and I."

I swallowed and looked at my watch. We were still a good two hours away from takeoff time.

"No, Doctor, you'll have to answer me. Shall we try it?"

I could still stall, though I was not hopeful that it would help me much. "I don't understand your motives, Dr. Naysmith. What do you want to try it *for*? The Chandalese are satisfied with their system. They won't thank you for trying to upset it. And where's the profit? I can't see any."

"What kind of profit are you talking about?" Naysmith said, almost abstractedly.

"Well . . . I don't know; that's what I'm asking you. It seems to me you shouldn't lack for money by now. And as for honor, you're up to your eyebrows in that already, and after Bbenaf you'll have much more. And yet you seem to be proposing to throw all that away for a moribund world you never heard of until tonight. And your life, too. They would kill you instantly down there if they knew what you had in mind."

"I don't plan to tell the ruling class, whatever that is, what I have in mind," Naysmith said. "I have that much sense. As for my motives . . . they're properly my own. But I can satisfy your curiosity a little. I know what you see when you look at me: a society doctor. It's not an unusual opinion. My record supports it. Isn't that true?"

I didn't nod, but my silence must have given my assent.

"Yes, it's true, of course. And if I had excuses, I wouldn't give a damn for your opinion – or for Chandala. But you see, I don't. I not only know what the opinion of me is, but *I share it myself*. Now I see a chance to change that opinion of me; not yours, but mine. Does that help you any?"

161

It did. Every man has his own Holy Grail. Naysmith had just identified his.

"I wish you luck."

"But you won't go along?"

"No," I said, miserable, yet defiantly sure that there were *no* good reasons why I should join Naysmith's quest – not even the reason that it could not succeed without me and my field kit. It could not succeed *with* me, either; and my duty lay with the ship, until the day when I might sight my own Grail, whatever that might be. All the same, that one word made me feel like an assassin.

But it did not surprise Naysmith. He had had the good sense to expect nothing else. Whatever the practical notions that had sprung into his head in the last hour or so, and I suppose they were many, he must have known all his life – as we all do – that Grail-hunting is essentially the loneliest of hobbies.

He made himself wholly unpopular on the bridge, which up to now had barely known he was aboard, wangling a ship's gig and a twenty-four-hour delay during which he could be force-fed the language of the nearest city-state by a heuristics expert, and then disembarked. The arrangement was that we were to pick him up on our next cruise, a year from now.

If he had to get off the planet before then, he could go into orbit and wait; he had supplies enough. He also had his full field medical kit, including a space suit. Since it is of the nature of Chandalese political geography to shift without notice, he agreed to base himself on the edge of a volcanic region which we could easily identify from space, yet small enough so that we wouldn't have to map it to find the gig.

Then he left. Everything went without incident (he told me later) until he entered the city-state of Gandu, whose language he had and where our embassy was. He had of course been told that the Chandalese, though humanoid, are three times as tall as Earthmen, but it was a little unnerving all the same to walk among them. Their size suited their world, which was a good twelve thousand miles in diameter. Surprisingly, it was not very dense, a fact nobody had been able to explain, since it was obviously an Earthlike planet; hence there was no gravitational impediment to growing its natives very large, and grow large they did. He would have to do much of his doctoring here on a stepladder, apparently.

The chargé d'affaires at the embassy, like those of us on ship, did his best to dissuade Naysmith.

"I don't say that you can't do something about the situation here," he said. "Very likely you can. But you'll be meddling with their social structure. Public health here is politics, and vice versa. The Heart stars — "

"Bother the Heart stars," Naysmith said, thereby giving the chargé d'affaires the worst fright he had had in years. "If it can be done, it ought to be done. And the best way to do it is to go right to the worst trouble spot."

"That would be Iridu, down the river some fifteen miles," the chargé d'affaires said. "Dying out very rapidly. But it's proscribed, as all those places are."

"Criminal. What about language?"

"Oh, same as here. It's one of three cities that spoke the same tongue. The third one is dead."

"Where do I go to see the head man?"

"To the sewer. He'll be there."

Naysmith stared.

"Well, I'm sorry, but that's the way things are. When you came through the main plaza here, did you see two tall totem poles?"

"Yes."

"The city totems always mark the local entrance to the Grand Sewer of Chandala, and the big stone building behind them is always where the priest-chief lives. And I'm warning you, Dr. Naysmith, he won't give you the time of day."

Naysmith did not bother to argue any more. It seemed

163

to him that no matter how thoroughly a chieftain may subscribe to a political system, he becomes a rebel when it is turned against him – especially if as a consequence he sees his people dying all around him. He left, and went downriver, on a vessel rather like a felucca.

He had enough acumen to realize very early that he was being trailed. One of the two Chandalese following him looked very like a man who had been on duty at the embassy. He did not let it bother him, and in any event, they did not seem to follow him past the gates of Iridu.

He found the central plaza easily enough – that is to say, he was never lost; the physical act of getting through the streets was anything but easy, though he was towing his gear on an antigrav unit. They were heaped with refuse and bodies. Those who still lived made no attempt to clear away the dead or help the dying, but simply sat in the doorways and moaned. The composite sound thrummed through the whole city. Now and then he saw small groups scavenging for food amid all the garbage; and quite frequently he saw individuals drinking from puddles. This last fact perplexed him particularly, for the chargé d'affaires had told him plainly that Chandala boasted excellent water-supply systems.

The reception of the chief-priest was hostile enough, more so than Naysmith had hoped, yet less than the chargé d'affaires had predicted – at least at first. He was obviously sick himself, and seemingly had not bathed in a long time, nor had any of his attendants; but as long as all Naysmith wanted was information, he was grudgingly willing to give it.

"What you observe are the Articles of the Law and their consequences," he said. "Because of high failures before the gods, Iridu and all its people have been abased to the lowest caste; and since it is not meet that people of this caste speak the same tongue as the Exalted, the city is proscribed."

"I can understand that," Naysmith said, guardedly.

164

"But why should that prevent you from taking any care of yourselves? Drinking from puddles — "

"These are the rules for our caste," the priest-chief said. "Not to wash; not to eat aught less than three days old; not to aid the sick or bury the dead. Drinking from puddles is graciously allowed us."

There was no apparent ironic intention in the last sentence. Naysmith said, "Graciously?"

"The water in the city's plumbing now comes directly from the Grand Sewer. The only other alternative is the urine of the anah, but that is for holy men doing penance for the people."

This was a setback. Without decent water he would be sadly handicapped, and obviously what came out of the faucets was not under the control of the doomed city.

"Well, we'll manage somehow. Rain barrels should serve for the time being; I can chlorinate them for you. But it's urgent to start cleaning things up; otherwise, I'll never be able to keep up with all the new cases. Will you help me?"

The priest-chief looked blank. "We can help no one any more, little one."

"You could be a big help. I can probably stop this plague for you, with a few willing hands."

The priest-chief stood up, shakily, but part of his shakiness was black rage. "To break the rules of caste is the highest of failures before the gods," he said. "We are damned to listen to such counsels! Kill him!"

Naysmith was fool enough to pause to protest. Only the fact that most of the gigantic soldiers in the chamber were clumsy with disease, and unused to dealing with so small an object as he, got him out of the building alive. He was pursued to the farther gate of Iridu by a shambling and horrible mob, all the more frightening because there was hardly a healthy creature in its rank.

Outside, he was confronted by a seemingly trackless jungle. He plunged in at hazard, and kept going blindly until he could no longer hear the noise of the pack; evidently they had stopped at the gate. He could thank the proscription of the city-nation for that.

On the other hand, he was lost.

Of course, he had his compass, which might help a little. He did not want to go westward, which would take him back to the river, but also into the vicinity of Iridu again. Besides, his two trackers from Gandu might still be lurking at the west gate, and this time their hostility might be a good deal more active. Striking north-northwest toward Gandu itself was open to the same objection. There seemed to be nothing for it but to go north-northeast, in the hope of arriving at the field of fumaroles and hot springs where his ship was, there to take thought.

He was still utterly determined to try again; shaken though he was, he was convinced that this first failure was only a matter of tactics. But he did have to get back to the ship.

He pushed forward through the wiry tangle. It made it impossible for him to follow a straight compass course; he lost hours climbing and skirting and hacking, and began to worry about the possibility of spending the night in this wilderness. With the thought, there was a sodden thump behind him, and he was stopped as though he had run into a wall. Then there was a diminishing crackle and bumping over his head.

What was holding him back, he realized after a moment, was the tow to his gear. He backtracked. The gear was lying on the moist ground. Some incredibly tough vine had cut the antigrav unit free of it; the other sound he heard had been the unit fighting its way skyward.

Now what? He could not possibly drag all this weight. It occurred to him that he might put on the space suit; that would slow him a good deal, but it would also protect him from the underbrush, which had already slashed him pretty painfully. The rest of the load – a pack and two oxygen bottles – would still be heavy, but maybe not impossibly so.

He got the suit on, though it was difficult without help, and lumbered forward again. It was exhausting, even with the suit's air conditioning to help, but there was nothing he could do about that. At least, if he had to sleep in the jungle, the suit might also keep out vermin, and some larger entities . . .

For some reason, however, the Chandalese forest seemed peculiarly free of large animals. Occasional scamperings and brief glimpses told of creatures which might have been a little like antelope, or like rabbits, but even these were scarce; and there were no cries of predators. This might have been because Chandalese predators were voiceless, but Naysmith doubted this on grounds of simple biology; it seemed more likely that most of the more highly organized wildlife of Chandala had long since been decimated by the plagues the owners of the planet cultivated as though they were ornamental gardens.

Late in the afternoon, the fates awarded him two lucky breaks. The first of these was a carcass, or rather, a shell. It was the greenish-brown carapace of some creature which, from its size, he first took to be the Chandalese equivalent of a huge land turtle, but on closer examination seemed actually to have been a good deal more like a tick. Well, if any planet had ticks as big as rowboats, it would be Chandala, that much was already plain even to Naysmith. In any event, the shell made an excellent skid for his gear, riding on its back through the undergrowth almost as though it had been designed for the task.

The second boon was the road. He did not recognize it as such at first, for it was much broken and overgrown, but on reflection he decided that this was all to the good; a road that had not been in use for a long time would be a road on which he would be unlikely to meet anybody. It would also not be likely to take him to any populated place, but it seemed to be headed more or less in the direction he wanted to go; and if it meandered a little, it could hardly impose upon him more detours than the jungle did.

He took off the space suit and loaded it into the skid, feeling almost cheerful.

It was dusk when he rounded the bend and saw the dead city. In the gathering gloom, it looked to be almost twice the size of Gandu, despite the fact that much of it had crumbled and fallen.

At its open gates stood the two Chandalese who had followed him downriver, leaning on broad-bladed spears as tall as they were.

Naysmith had a gun, and he did not hesitate.

Had he not recognized the face of the Chandalese from the chargé d'affaires' office, he might have assumed that the two guards were members of some savage tribe. Again, it seemed to him, he had been lucky.

It might be the last such stroke of luck. The presence of the guards testified, almost in letters of fire, that the Chandalese could predict his route with good accuracy – and the spears testified that they did not mean to let him complete it.

Again, it seemed to him that his best chance led through the dead city, protected while he was there by its proscription. He could only hope that the firelands lay within some reachable distance of the city's other side.

The ancient gate towered over him like the Lion Gate of Mycenae as remembered from some nightmare – fully as frowning as that narrow, heavy, tragedy-ridden breach, but more than five times as high. He studied it with sober respect, and perhaps even a little dread, before he could bring himself to step over the bodies of the guards and pass through it. When he did, he was carrying with him one of the broad-bladed fifteen-foot spears, because, he told himself, you never could tell when such a lever might come in handy . . . and because, instinctively, he believed (though he later denied it) that no stranger could pass under that ancient arch without one.

The Atridae, it is very clear, still mutter in their sleep not far below the surface of our waking minds, for all that we no longer allow old Freud to cram our lives back into the straitjackets of those old religious plays. Perhaps one of the changes in us that the Heart stars await is the extirpation of these last shadows of Oedipus, Elektra, Agamemnon, and all those other dark and bloody figures, from the way we think.

Or maybe not. There are still some forty thousand years to go. If after that they tell us that that was one of the things they were waiting for, we probably won't understand what they're talking about.

Carrying the spear awkwardly and towing his belongings behind him in the tick shell, Naysmith plodded toward the center of the dead city. There was nothing left in the streets but an occasional large bone; one that he stumbled over fell promptly to shivers and dust. The scraping noise of his awkward sledge echoed off the fronts of the leaning buildings; otherwise, there was no sound but the end-stopped thuds of his footfalls, and an occasional bluster of evening wind around the tottering, flaking cornices far above his bent head.

In this wise he came draggingly at last into the central plaza, and sat down on a drum of a fallen stone pillar to catch his breath. It was now almost full dark, so dark that nothing cast a shadow any more; instead, the night seemed to be soaking into the ground all around him. There would be, he knew already, no stars; the atmosphere of Chandala was too misty for that. He had perhaps fifteen minutes more to decide what he was going to do.

As he mopped his brow and tried to think, something rustled behind him. Freezing, he looked carefully over his shoulder, back toward the way he had come. Of course he saw nothing; but in this dead silence a sound like that was easy to interpret.

They were still following him. For him, this dead city was not a proscripted sanctuary. Or if it ever had been, it was no longer, since he had killed the two guards.

He stood up, as soundlessly as he could. All his muscles were aching; he felt as soft and helpless as an overripe melon. The shuffling noise stopped at once.

They were already close enough to see him!

He knew that he could vanish quickly enough into any of the tomblike buildings around him, and evade them for a while as deftly as any rat. They probably knew this labyrinth little better than he did, and the sound of their shuffling did not suggest that there were many of them – surely not a large enough force to search a whole city for a man only a third as big as a Chandalese. And they would have to respect taboos that he could scamper past out of simple ignorance.

But if he took that way, he would have to abandon his gear. He could carry his medical kit easily enough, but that was less important to him now than the space suit and its ancillary oxygen bottles – both heavy and clumsy, and both, furthermore, painted white. As long as he could drag them with him in the tick shell, their whiteness would be masked to some extent; but if he had to run with them, he would surely be brought down.

In the last remains of the evening, he stood cautiously forward and inched the sledge toward the center of the plaza, clenching the spear precariously against his side under one armpit, his gun in his other hand. Behind him, something went, *scuffle . . . rustle . . .*

As he had seen on arrival, the broad-mouthed well in the center of the plaza, before the house of the dead and damned priest-chief, was not flanked by the totems he had been taught to expect. Where they should be jutted only two gray and splintered stumps, as though the poles had been pushed over by brute force and toppled into the abyss. On the other side of the well, a stone beast – an anah? – stared forever downward with blind eyes, ready to rend any soul who might try to clamber up again from Hell.

170

As it might try to do; for a narrow, rail-less stone stairway, slimy and worn, spiralled around the well into the depths.

Around the mouth of the well, almost impossible to see, let alone interpret, in the last glimmers, was a series of bas-reliefs, crudely and hastily cut; he could detect the rawness of the sculpturing even under the weathering of the stone and the moss.

He went cautiously down the steps a little way to look at them. With no experience whatsoever of Chandalese graphic conventions, he knew that he had little chance of understanding them even had he seen them in full daylight. Nevertheless, it was clear that they told a history . . . and, it seemed to him, a judgment. This city had been condemned, and its totems toppled, because it had been carrying on some kind of congress with the Abyss.

He climbed back to the surface of the plaza, pulling his nose thoughtfully. They were still following him, that was sure. But would they follow him down there? It might be a way to get to the other side of the dead city which would promise him immunity – or at least, a temporary sanctuary of an inverted kind.

He did not delude himself that he could live down there for long. He would have to wear the space suit again, and breathe nothing but the oxygen in the white bottles. He could still keep by him the field medical kit with which he had been planning to re-enrich his opinion of himself, and save a planet; but even with this protection he could not for long breathe the air and drink the water of the pit. As for food, that hardly mattered, because his air and water would run out much sooner.

Let it be said that Naysmith was courageous. He donned the space suit again, and began the descent, lowering his tick-shell coracle before him on a short, taut tether. Bump, bump, bump went the shell down the steps ahead of him, teetering on its back ridge, threatening to slip sidewise and fall into the well at every irregularity in the slimy old

171

platforms. Then he would stop in the blackness and wait until he could no longer hear it rocking. Then down again: bump, bump, bump; step, step, step. Behind him, the butt of the spear scraped against the wall; and once the point lodged abruptly in some chink and nearly threw him.

He had his chest torch going, but it was not much help; the slimy walls of the well seemed to soak up the light, except for an occasional delusive reflection where a rill of seepage oozed down amid the nitre. Down, down, down.

After some centuries, he no longer expected to reach the bottom. There was nothing left in his future but this painful descent. He was still not frightened; only numb, exhausted, beyond caring about himself, beyond believing in the rest of the universe.

Then the steps stopped, sending him staggering in the suit. He touched the wall with a glove – he imagined that he could feel its coldness, though of course he could not – and stood still. His belt radios brought him in nothing but a sort of generalized echo, like running water.

Of course. He flashed the chest light around, and saw the Grand Sewer of Chandala.

He was standing on what appeared to be a wharf made of black basalt, over the edge of which rushed the black waters of an oily river, topped with spinning masses of soapy froth. He could not see the other side, nor the roof of the tunnel it ran in – only the sullen and ceaseless flood, like a cataract of ink. The wharf itself had evidently been awash not long since, for there were still pools standing sullenly wherever the black rock had been worn down; but now the surface of the river was perhaps a foot below the level of the dock.

He looked up. Far aloft, he saw a spot of blue-black sky about the size of a pea, and gleaming in it, one reddish star. Though he was no better judge of distance than any other surgeon or any other man who spends his life doing close work, he thought he was at least a mile beneath the surface. To clamber back up there would be utterly beyond him.

But why a wharf? Who would be embarking on this

sunless river, and why? It suggested that the river might go toward some other inhabited place . . . or some place that had once been inhabited. Maybe the Chandalese had been right in condemning the city to death for congress with the pit – and if that Other Place were inhabited even now, it was probably itself underground, and populated by whatever kind of thing might enjoy and prosper by living in total darkness by the side of a sewer —

There was an ear-splitting explosion to Naysmith's right, and something struck his suit just under his armpit. He jerked his light toward the sound, just in time to see fragments of rock scampering away across the wet wharf, skidding and splashing. A heavier piece rolled eccentrically to the edge of the dock and dropped off into the river. Then everything was motionless again.

He bent and picked up the nearest piece. It was part of one of the stones of the staircase.

There was no sanctuary, even here; they were following him down. In a few moments it might occur to them to stone him on purpose; the suit could stand that, but the helmet could not. And above all, he had to keep his air pure.

He had to go on. But there was no longer any walkway; only the wharf and the sewer. Well, then, that way. Grimly he unloaded the tick shell and lowered it into the black water, hitching its tether to a basalt post. Then, carefully, he ballasted it with the pack and the oxygen bottles. It rocked gently in the current, but the ridge along its back served as a rudimentary keel; it would be stable, more or less.

He sat down on the edge of the wharf and dangled his feet into his boat while he probed for the bottom of the river with the point of the spear. The point caught on something after he had thrust nearly twelve feet of the shaft beneath the surface; and steadying himself with this, he transferred his weight into the coracle and sat down.

Smash! Another paving stone broke on the dock. A splinter, evidently a large one, went whooshing past his helmet and dropped into the sewer. Hastily, he jerked the

173

loop of the tether off the basalt post, and poled himself hard out into the middle of the torrent.

The wharf vanished. The shell began to turn round and round. After several minutes, during which he became deathly seasick, Naysmith managed to work out how to use the blade of the spear as a kind of steering oar; if he held it hard against one side of the shell at the back, and shifted the shaft with the vagaries of the current, he could at least keep his frail machine pointed forward.

There was no particular point in steering it any better than that, since he did not know where he was going.

The chest light showed him nothing except an occasional glimpse of a swiftly passing tunnel wall, and after a while he shut it off to conserve power, trusting his sense of balance to keep his shell headed forward and in the middle of the current. Then he struck some obstacle which almost upset him; and though he fought himself back into balance again, the shell seemed sluggish afterwards. He put on the light and discovered that he had shipped so much of the slimy water that the shell was riding only a few inches above the rolling river.

He ripped the flap of his pack open and found a cup to bail with. Thereafter, he kept the light on.

After a while, the noise of the water took on a sort of hissing edge. He hardly noticed it at first; but soon it became sharp, like the squeak of a wet finger on the edge of a glass, and then took on deeper tones until it made the waters boil like the noise of a steam whistle. Turning the belt radio down did him very little good; it dropped the volume of the sound, but not its penetrating quality.

Then the coracle went skidding around a long bend and light burst over him.

He was hurtling past a city, fronted by black basalt docks like the one he had just quitted, but four or five times more extensive. Beyond these were ruins, as far as he could see, tumbled and razed, stark in the unwavering flare of five tall, smokeless plumes of gas flames which towered amid the tumbled stones. It was these five fountains of blue-white fire, as tall as sequoias, which poured out the vast organ-diapason of noise he had heard in the tunnel.

They were probably natural, though he had never seen anything like them before. The ruins, much more obviously, were not; and for them there was no explanation. Broken and aged though they were, the great carved stones still preserved the shapes of geometrical solids which could not possibly have been reassembled into any building Naysmith could imagine, though as a master surgeon he had traded all his life on structural visualization. The size of the pieces did not bother him, for he had come to terms with the fact that the Chandalese were three times as tall as men, but their shapes were as irrational as the solid geometry of a dream.

And the crazy way in which the city had been dumped over, as though something vast and stupid had sat down in the middle of it and lashed a long heavy tail, did not suggest that its destroyers had been Chandalese either.

Then it was gone. He clung to his oar, keeping the coracle pointed forward. He did not relish the thought of going on to a possible meeting with the creatures who had razed that city; but obviously there had been no hope for him in its ruins. It dwindled and dimmed, and then he went wobbling around a bend and even its glow vanished from the sides of the tunnel.

As he turned that corner, something behind him shrieked, cutting through the general roar of noise like a god in torture. He shrank down into the bottom of the boat, almost losing his hold on the spear. The awful yell must have gone on for two or three minutes, utterly overpowering every echo. Then, gradually, it began to die, at first into a sort of hopeless howl, then into a series of raw, hoarse wails, and at last into a choked mixture of weeping and giggling . . . oh! oooh! . . . whee! . . . oh, oh, oh . . . whee! . . . which made Naysmith's every hair stand on end. It was, obviously, only one of the high-pressure gas jets fluting over a rock lip.

Obviously.

After that he was glad to be back in the darkness, however little it promised. The boat bobbed and slithered in the midst of the flood. On turns it was washed against the walls and Naysmith poled it back into the center of the current as best he could with his break-bone spear, which kept knocking him about the helmet and ribs every time he tried to use it for anything but steering. Some of those collisions were inexplicably soft; he did not try to see why, because he was saving the chest light for bailing, and in any event he was swept by them too fast to look back.

Just under him gurgled the Grand Sewer of Chandala, a torrent of filth and pestilence. He floated down it inside his suit, Naysmith, master surgeon, a bubble of precarious life in a universe of corruption, skimming the entropy gradient clinging to the edges of a tick's carapace . . . and clinging to incorruption to the last.

Again, after a while, he saw light ahead, sullenly red at first, but becoming more and more orange as the boat swept on. For the first time he saw the limits of the tunnel, outlined ahead of him in the form of a broad arch. Could he possibly be approaching the surface? It did not seem possible; it was night up there – and besides, Chandalese daylight was nothing like this.

Then the tunnel mouth was behind him, and he was coasting on an enormous infernal sea.

The light was now a brilliant tangerine color, but he could not see where it came from; billowing clouds of mist rising from the surface of the sewage limited visibility to perhaps fifty feet. The current from the river was quickly dissipated, and the coracle began to drift sidewise; probing with the spear without much hope, he was surprised to touch bottom, and began to pole himself forward with the aid of his compass – though he had almost forgotten why it was that he had wanted to go in that direction.

The bottom was mucky, as was, of course, to be expected; pulling the spear out of it was tiring work. Far overhead in the mists, he twice heard an odd fluttering sound, rather like that of a tightly wound rubber band suddenly released, and once a measured flapping which seemed to pass quite low over his head; he saw nothing, however.

After half an hour he stopped poling to give himself five minutes' rest. Again he began to drift sidewise. Insofar as he could tell, the whole of this infernal deep seemed to be eddying in a slow circle.

Then a tall, slender shadow loomed ahead of him. He drove the spear into the bottom and anchored himself, watching intently, but the shadow remained fixed. Finally he pushed the shell cautiously toward it.

It was a totem pole, obviously very old; almost all its paint was gone, and the exposed wood was gray. There were others ahead; within a few moments he was in what was almost a forest of them, their many mute faces grinning and grimacing at him or staring hopelessly off into the mists. Some of them were canted alarmingly and seemed to be on the verge of falling into the ordure, but even with these he found it hard to set aside the impression that they were watching him.

There was, he realized slowly, a reason for this absurd, frightening feeling. The totems testified to something more than the deaths of uncountable thousands of Chandalese. They were witness also to the fact that this gulf was known and visited, at least by the priest-chief caste; obviously the driving of the poles in this abyss was the final ritual act of condemnation of a city-state. He was not safe from pursuit yet.

And what, he found himself wondering despite his desperation, could it possibly be all about – this completely deliberate, systematic slaughter of whole nations of one's fellow beings by pestilence contrived and abetted? It was

certainly not a form of warfare; *that* he might have understood. It was more like the extermination of the rabbits of
Australia by infecting them with a plague. He remembered
very dimly that the first settlers of North America had tried,
unsuccessfully, to spread smallpox among the Indians for
the same reason; but the memory seemed to be no help in
understanding Chandala.

Again he heard that rhythmic sound, now much closer,
and something large and peculiarly rubbery went by him,
almost on a level with his shoulders. At his sudden movement, it rose and perched briefly on one of the totems, just
too far ahead in the mist to be clearly visible.

He had not the slightest desire to get any closer to it, but
the current was carrying him that way. As he approached,
dragging the blade of the spear fruitlessly, the thing seemed
to fall off the pole, and with a sudden flap of wings – he could
just make out their spread, which seemed to be about four
feet – disappeared into the murk.

He touched his gun. It did not reassure him much. It
occurred to him that since this sea was visited, anything
that lived here might hesitate to attack him, but he knew
he could not count on that. The Chandalese might well
have truces with such creatures which would not protect
Naysmith for an instant. It was imperative to keep going,
and if possible, to get out.

The totem poles were beginning to thin out. He could see
high-water marks on the remaining ones, which meant that
the underground ocean was large enough to show tides, but
he had no idea what size that indicated; for one thing, he
knew neither the mass nor the distance of Chandala's moon.
He did remember, however, that he had seen no tide marks
as he had entered the forest of idols, which meant that it
was ebbing now; and it seemed to him that the current was
distinctly faster than before.

He poled forward vigorously. Several times he heard the
flapping noise and the fluttering sounds again, and not
these alone. There were other noises. Some of them were

178

impossible to interpret, and some of them so suggestive that he could only pray that he was wrong about them. For a while he tried shutting the radio off, but he found the silence inside the helmet even less possible to endure, as well as cutting him off from possible cues to pursuit.

But the current continued to pick up, and shortly he noticed that he was casting a shadow into the shell before him. If the source of the light, whatever it was, was over the center of the sea, it was either relatively near the water or he had come a long distance; perhaps both.

Then there was a wall looming to his left side. Five more long thrusts with the spear, and there was another on his right. The light dimmed; the water ran faster.

He was back on a river again. By the time the blackness closed down the current was rushing, and once more he was forced to sit down and use the spear as a steering oar. Again ahead of him he heard the scream of gas jets.

Mixed with that sound was another noise, a prolonged roaring which at first completely baffled him. Then, suddenly, he recognized it; it was the sound of a great cataract.

Frantically, he flashed his light about. There was a ledge of sorts beside the torrent, but he was going so fast now that to make a leap for it would risk smashing his helmet. All the same, he had no choice. He thrust the skidding coracle toward the wall and jumped.

He struck fair, on his feet. He secured his balance in time to see the shell swept away, with his pack and spare oxygen bottles.

For a reason he cannot now explain, this amused him.

This, as Naysmith chooses to tell it, is the end of the meaningful part of the story, though by no means the end of his travails; these he dismisses as "scenery." As his historian, I can't be quite so offhand about them, but he has supplied me with few details to go by.

He found the cataract, not very far ahead; evidently, he had jumped none too soon. As its sound had suggested, it was a monster, leaping over an underground cliff which he guesses must have been four or five miles high, into a cavern which might have been the Great Gulf itself. He says, and I think he is right, that we now have an explanation for the low density of Chandala: If the rest of it has as much underground area as the part he saw, its crust must be extremely porous. By this reckoning, the Chandalese underworld must have almost the surface area of Mars.

It must have seemed a world to itself indeed to Naysmith, standing on the rim of that gulf and looking down at its fire-filled floor. Where the cataract struck, steam rose in huge billows and plumes, and with a scream which forced him to shut off the radio at once. Occasionally the ground shook faintly under his feet.

Face to face with Hell, Naysmith found reason to hope. This inferno, it seemed to him, might well underlie the region of hot springs, geysers, and fumaroles toward which he had been heading from the beginning; and if so, there should be dead volcanic funnels through which he might escape to the surface. This proved to be the case; but first he had to pick his way around the edge of the abyss to search for one, starting occasional rockslides, the heat blasting through his helmet, and all in the most profound and unnatural silence. If this is scenery, I prefer not to be offered any more scenic vacations.

"But on the way, I figured it out," Naysmith told me. "Rituals don't grow without a reason – especially not rituals involving a whole culture. This one has a reason that I should have been the first to see – or any physician should. You, too."

"Thanks. But I *don't* see it. If the Heart stars do, they aren't telling."

"They must think it's obvious," Naysmith said. "It's

eugenics. Most planets select for better genes by controlling breeding. The Chandalese do it by genocide. They force their lower castes to kill themselves off."

"Ugh. Are you sure? Is it scientific? I don't see how it could be, under the circumstances."

"Well, I don't have all the data. But I think a really thorough study of Chandalese history, with a statistician to help, would show that it is. It's also an enormously dangerous method, and it may wind up with the whole planet dead; that's the chance they're taking, and I assume they're aware of it."

"Well," I said, "assuming that it does work, I wouldn't admit a planet that 'survived' by that method into any federation *I* ran."

"No," Naysmith said soberly. "Neither would I. And there's the rub, you see, because the Heart stars *will*. That's what shook me. I may have been a lousy doctor – and don't waste your breath denying it, you know what I mean – but I've been giving at least lip service to all our standard humanitarian assumptions all my life, without ever examining them. What the Chandalese face up to, and we don't, is that death is now and has always been *the* drive wheel of evolution. They not only face up to it, they *use* it.

"When I was down there in the middle of that sewer, I was in the middle of my own *Goetzendaemmerung* – the twilight of the idols that Nietzsche speaks of. I could see all the totems of my own world, of my own life, falling into the muck . . . shooting like logs over the brink into Hell. And it was then that I knew I couldn't be a surgeon any more."

"Come now," I said. "You'll get over it. After all, it's just another planet with strange customs. There are millions of them."

"You weren't there," Naysmith said, looking over my shoulder at nothing. "For you, that's all it is. For me . . . 'No other taste shall change this.' Don't you see? All planets are Chandalas. It's not just that Hell is real. The laws that run it are the laws of life everywhere."

His gaze returned to me. It made me horribly uneasy.

"What was it Mephistopheles said? 'Why, this is Hell, nor am I out of it.' The totems are falling all around us as we sit here. One by one, Rosenbaum; one by one."

And that is how we lost Naysmith. It would have been easy enough to say simply that he had a desperate experience on a savage planet and that it damaged his sanity, and let it go at that. But it would not be true. I would dismiss it that way myself if I could.

But I cannot bring myself to forget that the Heart stars classify Chandala as a civilized world.